To:
Super Pa
- More powerful
a two-edged sword!
- Leaps Covid without
a single vaccine!

Christ's blessings,

Steve

Backlash

A Chronicle of the Avenging Angel

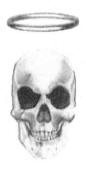

Steve Stranghoener

For the silent majority.

Part One:

Then Came Bronson

"*If the police don't defend us, maybe we ought to do it ourselves.*"

(*PAUL KERSEY* IN *DEATH WISH*)

Chapter 1:

I didn't know Michael Wyatt from Adam even though we hailed from the same St. Louis suburb and graduated from the same high school albeit more than ten years apart. At first, I was only acquainted with his reputation as an anonymous hero or, perhaps more aptly put by some, an anti-hero. Otherwise nameless, I tabbed him and the media ran with the moniker of Avenging Angel for exploits more often deemed vigilantism than heroism.

Although months passed before our introduction, he backfilled everything I'd missed once he coaxed me into serving as his intermediary to the press. This allowed him to protect his identity while telling his side of things through me. After I earned his trust, he opened up to me and allowed me to gain an insight into his motivations. As our relationship blossomed, my unique position as an insider gave a much-needed shot in the arm to my broadcasting career. More on that later but enough about me.

AA, as he came to be known, never had any intention of becoming a crime fighter. Neither he nor anyone in his family had a background in law enforcement or the military. Although a pretty talented jock in his youth and still somewhat physically imposing at six-foot-one and two-hundred pounds of well-toned muscle; at fifty-two, age wasn't working in his favor. As for work, his career as an executive at a Fortune 100 company didn't contribute much toward his new vocation.

It came about mostly by accident or perhaps providence one afternoon after lunch in downtown St. Louis as he strolled back to his car in a parking garage practically devoid of people. He paid no attention to the four young men well across the way until a sudden movement caught his eye. Their pace quickened as they sped toward another lone customer walking with his back to them. An older, rather feeble-looking fellow was oblivious as they swept up on him from behind like a pestilence. The fellow at the head of the pack reared back and cocked his arm behind his shoulder and unleashed his fist in a long, looping arc that connected flush to the side of the unsuspecting man's head with a sickening thunk.

He never saw it coming and collapsed to the pavement in a heap like a sack full of doorknobs. The miscreants hooted, hollered and high-fived as if they'd just scored the winning touchdown in the Super Bowl. Blood oozed from the nose and mouth of the limp, lifeless body. For all they knew, he could have been dead but there was no remorse. They encircled him and taunted him with crude racial invectives while repeatedly thrusting their index fingers at him like accusatory pistons.

From about thirty yards away, Michael Wyatt reflexively yelled, "Hey!"

They turned his way and angrily shouted while disparaging his race and lineage; accusing him of incest in the crudest vernacular.

They started to tread in his direction but instead of retreating to safety, Wyatt advanced toward them. Surprised, they turned and ran toward the exit laughing and cheering while unleashing a mostly unintelligible tirade of foul insults. Michael started to pursue them but stopped to tend to the unconscious victim while dialing 911. He stayed long enough to see the poor man hauled away in an ambulance and then gave a report to the police. They informed him that the old gentleman had been a victim of something called the knockout game.

According to the police, this vile game was all too popular among young street thugs who considered it some kind of sick recreational activity. They sought out weak and helpless victims for ambush from sneak attacks that rendered them completely defenseless. The object was simple: to score a knockout. Anything less would be considered an embarrassment. Never mind that the sitting duck might get killed in the process. That's what whitey deserved anyway, according to their hateful philosophy.

Wyatt explained to me later that this served as a turning point. This wasn't an outrage seen over cable news or social media. He was an eyewitness to mindless savagery that struck him as pure evil. This compelled him to do something totally out of character. He actually went to the hospital to check on the well-being of the old gentleman. Sadly, the poor soul was in a vegetative state and never regained consciousness before dying days later. To make matters worse, Wyatt learned from grieving family members that the old fellow had just received a citizenship award for his longtime service as a basketball coach and mentor to underprivileged, inner city youths. This gross injustice received nothing but crickets from the media.

As a busy executive, Michael Wyatt didn't have time to dwell on the tragedy. The company demanded virtually all of his waking hours. He didn't mind though, partly because of his dedication but also due to his circumstances. His wife had divorced him years before while citing irreconcilable differences, not the least of which was his inability to give her children. What he considered as her betrayal devastated him so much that he avoided anything beyond casual relationships with the fairer sex. Instead, he became a stoic loner, wedded to the job while substituting career success for intimacy and family ties.

Depending on one's point of view, what happened next was an unbelievably unfortunate coincidence or perhaps again providence. The new CEO of the company where Michael Wyatt worked so diligently launched a crusade that put politics and ideology above business. Like many large corporations and their leaders in the loony, upside-down world of 2020, this thirtysomething, woke white guy tried to assuage his guilt and signal his self-proclaimed virtue by jumping on the progressive bandwagon with both feet. He went so far as to send an email to each and every one of the tens of thousands of employees across the country. Therein, he declared that if there was anyone within the company who wasn't outraged by the blatant social injustice and systemic racism running rampant in American, then perhaps they should look for work elsewhere.

Michael, being an old-school, self-reliant, patriotic American who had been raised to respect traditional, Christian values, couldn't swallow such a full-frontal assault on his liberty. This had been building up in him for years but he'd always kept his nose to the grindstone while remaining part of the silent, compliant majority. However, this was too much. He'd given his life and whole heart to this company. Now, some misguided, pampered little punk was spitting in his face and blatantly censoring everything that he and many other people sincerely believed in.

You might say he snapped and flew off the handle in the heat of the moment. However, the truth was that he calmly took stock of his standing before responding. Although the timing wasn't ideal, his portfolio reflected what he called kiss-my-ass-money. Between his pension, 401k, stock options and other savings, he could get by without working if he could bridge the three-year gap until he turned fifty-five and became pension-eligible. With that in his hip pocket, he went back and read the email over again several times before hitting reply all.

The email he sent to every employee up to and including the CEO was a classic. After he extolled the virtues of free-market capitalism and America's Godly heritage, he gave the CEO a piece of his mind that included the words "impudent, clueless and fascist." He sealed the deal by exposing his old-school bona fides when he dipped into his late father's lexicon to personally insult the boss. Wyatt started by declaring that the CEO was "full of condensed weasel poop" and concluded with a direct shot across the bow. "If you don't like me expressing my First Amendment rights, then you can pucker up and kiss my butt on the corner of Wall and Broad!" His old man had actually used a local landmark from back in the day, Grand and Olive, but Michael substituted a much more famous intersection to drive the point home.

Michael Wyatt hadn't lost his mind. He knew that he'd be fired but had also read the fine print in his employment contract. Although he could be terminated for cause, as an executive, the company would have to grace his exit with some lovely parting gifts. No doubt, his was a bold move but one based on principle more so than emotion. Additionally, it gave him great satisfaction in knowing that, by falling on his sword so defiantly, he'd boost the morale of thousands of other employees who were also sick of the oppressive BS but too vulnerable to do anything about it.

Everything went according to Hoyle until Murphy's Law gummed up the works. All Michael had to do was to secure work for the next three years. He realized that the notoriety he'd gained wouldn't help, especially with his old company doing everything possible to defame his reputation. Accordingly, he assumed he'd have to settle for a lessor position with another company. However, he didn't anticipate that the economy would be shut down due to a pandemic and, thus, had to recalibrate.

Partly to keep some pocket change flowing in and also just to stay busy to ward off stir craziness, Michael Wyatt, the erstwhile respected business executive, took a job as a security guard. He convinced himself it was just temporary. The pay was miniscule by comparison but it included some healthcare benefits. That was worth more than his wages because paying for COBRA would have cost an arm and a leg and the last thing he wanted was to sign up for Obamacare: lousy coverage at a high price. He considered going without health insurance since he was fit as a fiddle but didn't want to tempt fate.

Wyatt rightly attributed his good health to a mostly healthy diet and plenty of regular exercise. Once out of college, he'd continued to participate in team sports like touch football, basketball and softball to stay active and fit. Even when the rigors of climbing the career ladder consumed much of his time, he still maintained a pedantically consistent workout regimen. Weight training one day was always followed by cardio the next with miles and miles of roadwork.

In his early forties, when team sports became virtually impossible due to work and marriage responsibilities that swamped his pals, he took a lone wolf approach and decided, on a lark, to take karate lessons. He wasn't into it so much for the martial arts as he was for the great workout it provided. The calisthenics were awesome and all the stretching helped immensely with maintaining flexibility. Wyatt stuck with it through white, yellow, orange, green, blue and brown belts. Having gone that far, he even achieved the Nidan or second-degree black belt level before calling it quits, at least formally. At fifty, he opted to maintain his skills individually. The only regret was forfeiting regular sparring opportunities but he still fed his competitive nature by occasionally entering local tournaments.

Wyatt had never had occasion to use his special skills outside the dojo. Still, he relished the confidence his training instilled in him and felt quite capable if circumstances ever required self-defense. Whenever he did push-ups, he balled his fists and placed the first two knuckles of each hand on the hard floor to hone the striking surface and strengthen his wrists for impact. His ab workout was extensive and varied to maintain a strong core; so important for delivering kicks and punches. When a buddy was available, he'd ask his partner to straddle his legs and deliver strong blows to his stomach each time it contracted with a cruncher. Little did he know that his years of toil and sacrifice would soon pay off.

Although working a security detail was lonely and oftentimes boring, it had a few side benefits. If provided plenty of time to scour the job market regularly. He appreciated the freedom this afforded but it became depressing when his employment searches came up empty time and again. Beyond getting way too familiar with *Monster* and *Indeed.com*, Michael's reduced responsibilities allowed him to take his workouts up a notch without having to squeeze them in at bizarre hours like he'd done as a busy executive. Still he felt underwhelmed and sought new ways to challenge himself.

At first, he tried to resist what he considered a crazy notion. *What could he do to help people like that poor man who'd been murdered at the hands of savage thugs without the conscience of a beagle? Should he join the police force? Nah, today they were more in need of protection than the citizenry. Plus, in St. Louis, local authorities and prosecutors openly persecuted the cops while siding with the criminals. How about the military? Boot camp would be no problem but, heck, it was still a young man's game.* He pushed such silliness out of his brain.

No matter how hard he tried, he couldn't get that poor, old man off his mind. This was made even more difficult by the daily images of violence coming across the news and social media. He remedied the situation by avoiding cable news and *Facebook* altogether. However, one sleepless night, insanity got a boost when Michael tuned into *TCM* to pass the time. They just so happened to be showing all five *Death Wish* movies in consecutive order. In his fragile state of mind, Michael Wyatt got sucked in almost immediately as *Paul Kersey*, played by Charles Bronson, sought to avenge the murder of his wife and rape of his daughter.

Like a hardcore insomniac, Wyatt remained glued to the TV as the entire marathon aired. What started as a personal vendetta became a crusade of epic proportions as *Kersey* sought to secure justice for an entire city. Once past the first two installments, it would have been easy to dismiss the last three movies as sophomoric lunacy except for a couple of things. Michael Wyatt could remember what New York City was like before the cavalry arrived in the person of Mayor Rudy Giuliani. Maybe these flicks exaggerated the extent of the crime and violence but it wasn't too far off. If that wasn't enough, all he had to do was turn on the news and take a gander at NYC today under Mayor Bill DeBlasio. Life under the left-wing loon was imitating art.

St. Louis wasn't far behind NYC. In fact, in some ways, it was worse but with fewer people packed in like the sardines in New York. This left Michael Wyatt with a dilemma. *What was he supposed to do, buy a gun and start prowling the streets at night?* He quickly dismissed this as a foolish fantasy induced by sleep-deprivation. Then, oddly enough, another weird coincidence occurred as he prepared to hit the sack for a few hours before daybreak. He pointed the remote and hit guide to see if anything was coming up that he should record. *TCM* seemed to be pushing a theme when he noticed they were also going to air the entire *Dirty Harry* series of films. What the heck! He pressed the little red button.

He was about to shut things down and head to the bedroom when he noticed something else on the guide. It was listed under the channel that featured classic TV shows from the 60s and 70s. This one was unfamiliar to him but the title caught his eye: *Then Came Bronson*. He hit the info button to see if Charles Bronson was featured. Turned out it was a bleeding-heart series that only lasted a year in 1969. It featured Michael Parks as a disillusioned journalist riding around the country on a motorcycle while helping random folks along the way. Wyatt disregarded it as liberal pabulum but couldn't get the title out of his mind: *Then Came Bronson*. Fictional NYC was in a shamble until Charles Bronson arrived in the person of *Paul Kersey*. Maybe St. Louis could use a little of the same.

Chapter 2:

Idle hands are the devil's workshop, or so they said. Michael Wyatt was beset with idle hands and an idle, wandering mind. As hard as he tried to occupy himself with other things, he couldn't help but identify with *Paul Kersey*. Sure, he was a vigilante who didn't respect the rule of law but hadn't his hand been forced by feckless authorities who'd left regular folks at the mercy of violent sociopaths? Weren't things even worse in reality today with supposed leaders siding with the bad guys? Right here in St. Louis, an insane prosecuting attorney was refusing to try cases brought by police men and women she disliked. Hardened felons were being released from jails and prisons due to the threat of COVID-19 while the same corrupt politicians insisted that everyone else wear masks and stay at home under virtual house arrest.

Logic, common sense and the memory of the knockout game wouldn't release Michael from its steely grip. Still, he couldn't bring himself to resort to vigilante justice. Instead, he settled for what, in his mind, seemed like a fair compromise. He'd take to the streets but strictly as an observer. If he ever came across another situation like the one in the parking garage, he'd alert the police. At least that's what he told himself.

Wyatt's circumstances were well-suited to his odd, new hobby. He'd sold his home in the suburbs. This served as a cost-cutting measure but was also a bulwark against loneliness. The place was way too big and empty. It served as a constant, painful reminder of how he and his ex-wife had originally planned to fill the place up with kids. After closing, he'd moved into a downtown condo conveniently located within walking distance of the office building where he worked as a security guard.

Michael Wyatt told me later that he felt like a fish out of water the first time he ventured out at night to casually patrol the area. It helped that the Cardinals were playing. This allowed him to be unobtrusive while observing the folks mingling outside the stadium and Ballpark Village. This didn't really serve much of a purpose though since there was heightened security in this area on game days. Common sense dictated that he'd have to venture further from the limelight to do any good but he couldn't bring himself to leave his comfort zone. It was unfamiliarity more than fear. The whole idea seemed so foreign to him.

After a few fruitless weeks, he was ready to dismiss his newfound passion as foolish; especially when the Cardinals left town for a road trip. The little bit of vibrancy they provided evaporated and the surrounding desolation crept in like a thick fog. When his nightly sojourns ceased, he was able to mostly bury the memories of the old man that had tormented him. Then, that persistent, annoying pest known as providence came calling again.

It was early evening when most people had left the building to head to their homes. Only a few dedicated stragglers remained. They reminded him of his days as a corporate workaholic. Boredom gripped him as he sat in front of a bank of mostly blank security monitors. Then some movement occurred to his far left. The camera on level one of the parking garage captured a group of skulking young men that seemed eerily familiar. He couldn't be sure but they looked a lot like the vile bunch that had beaten the old man to death. Wyatt stared intently as they displayed the same malevolent stealth by stalking inside a garage at the perfect time to prey upon some unfortunate loner.

Across the way from this pack of human jackals, Wyatt noticed some more movement. To his shock and dismay, the elevator doors were opening. He desperately hoped that the thugs wouldn't catch this but then realized that, unlike him, they'd be alerted by the dinging sound. Sure enough, they cocked their heads and smiled devilishly as they advanced toward their target. Dread clutched Michael as he recognized the person stepping from the elevator. It was that pretty, petite blonde from Human Resources that he'd admired from afar. She'd been on his radar for a while after he'd caught a glimpse of her in the cafeteria line. Adrenaline kicked in and he dialed 911 to alert the cops before rushing toward the exit to the parking garage.

His mind screamed, *hurry, hurry* as he frantically sped to rescue her. He knew from experience how swiftly they could mete out their barbarous savagery. In a panic, he stumbled and fell as he lurched into the elevator and crashed against the back wall with such force that it cracked the mirrored tile. He fretted silently as it seemed to take forever for each floor button to light up; *I know I'm going to be too late! Oh God, please don't let them get her!*

This time, the devil dogs made a tactical error by pausing to allow their salacious urges to overtake their penchant for mindless violence. Instead of knocking her out, the vicious thugs decided to sexually degrade their helpless victim. Michael Wyatt was strangely pleased to see that she had been forced to her knees by the other three while the ringleader prepared to sodomize the terrified woman. At least it bought some

17

valuable time and she wasn't lying dead in a heap as he'd feared.

Things got really tense when she broke free just long enough to rake her fingernails across his cheek leaving four deep, bloody trails. This enraged the startled thug so much that he vowed to kill the "white bee-otch" after he'd satisfied his prurient urges. The other three grabbed her roughly and forced her back to her knees. One slapped her viciously for good measure and stated that he'd be second in line. As he exited the elevator, this incensed Michael even more but at least it served to buy a few more precious seconds.

They were so caught up in a frenzy that they didn't notice the sound of the elevator over their victim's screams. Michael didn't say a word to alert them. Something deep in his brain must have clicked as if it were installing a pre-programmed app. All of his martial arts training kicked in as he hurtled toward them like a seek-and-destroy missile. He flung himself at the three who were holding her as if he were breaking down a wedge of opposing football players on a kickoff. They all went down in a heap like bowling pins.

The young lady gasped as she gathered herself, frozen in place and too shocked to do

anything other than observe in wonder. Michael
sprang back to his feet like a cat and turned
toward the fourth goon who produced a gleaming
knife with a deadly four-inch blade. As if he'd
been rehearsing this move for years, Michael
unleashed a perfect roundhouse kick that caught
the man flush on the back of his hand. The
crunching contact was so violent that the knife
flew almost twenty feet away and landed under a
parked car. It must have snapped several of the
delicate bones in the punk's pulverized paw
because he howled in pain.

He doubled over grasping his injured claw
and Michael seized the opportunity to thrust a
knee flush into his forehead. This caused him to
be flung backward in a violent arc. The former
knockout champ was unconscious before the back
of his head slammed into the pavement. By this
time, the other three were back to their feet but
stunned by what they'd just seen. Even at a three-
to-one advantage, they didn't like their odds
against the guy that had just flattened the toughest
mother in their little gang. With that, they
sprinted toward the exit while one of them
vowed, "We'll get you!" again making mention
of his race while denigrating his mother, as
appeared to be their habit.

Still pumped and not yet ready to give up the fight, Michael Wyatt yelled, "You think so? The cops will get you first after they flip this punk friend of yours! Yeah, wait and see! This guy will rat on you!"

His rage began to subside even before he turned away from the fleeing thugs. That's because he could hear the low sobbing behind him. His damsel in distress was no longer catatonic. Instead, she mercurially went through a wide range of feelings as her pent-up emotions gushed to be released. "I was so frightened!" More choking sobs convulsed her. "Nothing like this has ever happened to me before."

Michael moved in to sooth her by putting an arm around her shoulder. "Everything is okay now. There's nothing to be afraid of anymore."

She surprised him by throwing her arms around his neck and hugging him tightly; apparently, she was so grateful that she had no inhibitions about embracing a virtual stranger. In all of about forty-five seconds that seemed to last an eternity, sobs became sniffles and then disappeared altogether with one long sigh of relief. Finally composed, she removed herself to arms-length and then brushed at his uniform shirt as if removing the tear stains and wrinkles she'd caused. After wiping her eyes and straightening her beautiful, golden curls, she looked deep into Michael's eyes with sheer admiration and exclaimed, "You were amazing."

His face flushed red as he fumbled to respond, finally settling on, "Aw, it was nothing," to end the awkward silence. Immediately, he realized how silly this sounded but she didn't seem to mind. He recovered nicely with, "You were pretty amazing too the way you clawed that bum's face."

She acknowledged the compliment with a proud smile but quickly shifted the focus back to his heroics, "How can I ever thank you?"

He desperately wanted to say, *would you go out to dinner with me sometime*? However, he paused while worrying, *I'm probably fifteen years older than her; almost old enough to be her father.* Before he could respond, they were both distracted by moaning as the dethroned knockout champ came to and sat up groggily. Michael moved between him and the girl and prepared himself to dispatch the thug again, if necessary. Thankfully, no further intervention was required as two squad cars pulled into the garage. They gave the police a full report and were happy to hear them say they'd take perp to the station for questioning to gain the identity of the other three.

As Michael walked the young lady to her car, he gathered the courage to say, "I know we've seen each other around but we've never been formally introduced. I'm Michael Wyatt." He extended his hand in greeting.

She surprised him by gently pushing his hand away. Smiling coyly, she pointed out, "I think we've already gotten past a handshake." She didn't hug him again like before but clasped his face in both hands, stood on her tippy toes and kissed him on the forehead. Once flat-footed again, she demurely stated, "Nice to meet you Michael. I'm Sally Temple."

For a moment, Michael was tempted to crack a lame joke and pretend he heard her wrong and ask, *Shirley Temple*? Thankfully, he thought better of it. He figured she'd probably heard this stale line a million times. Or worse, she might not get it and he'd have to explain who Shirley Temple was, thus, unnecessarily highlighting their age difference.

Chapter 3:

One would have thought that Michael Wyatt's angst would have been satisfied after he avenged the old man's death. Especially since he had something even more intriguing to occupy his mind: Sally Temple. He was definitely consumed with the pretty, little gal from HR but it was more than her blonde curls, charming wit and sunny disposition. Michael couldn't forget how close she'd come to being ravaged by those four animals. After he'd personally encountered two such harrowing situations by mere chance within a few weeks, he wondered how many other people were facing similar dangers on a regular basis?

He could only surmise that something was very wrong out there. A virus from China had thrown the nation for a loop. Incredible, unthinkable changes were accepted without question by an American public that seemed to be hypnotized by fear. Businesses were shut down, schools were closed, sports were put on hold and everything normal was locked in suspended animation. Millions of people had lost their jobs through no fault of their own. Worst of all, this led to a rise in crime that was met with appeasement from many and, incredibly, encouragement by some in power. Our country had lost its moral compass. Had the pandemic somehow wiped out common sense?

Michael didn't want to think so but, apparently, the answer was yes, at least in St. Louis. Sally approached him at work one day and informed Michael that she'd been asked to go down to City Hall. She asked if he would accompany her. He was secretly thrilled by this invitation but tried to conceal his excitement. "Sure, if you think it would help."

It soon became clear that she wasn't using this situation as an excuse to pursue a romantic motive. "Something's bothering me. I could use some moral support from someone who was there and can back me up."

"What's the problem? Did they say something?"

"It's more of what they didn't say. I'm not clear as to what they want from me."

"Did you ask?"

"Yes, but they only said they wanted to discuss the case. They were so vague that it seemed they were hiding something. Plus, it wasn't the police but rather the Prosecutor's office."

Michael tried to put her at ease. "I'm sure they're just trying to build their case. They're probably being tight-lipped in order to avoid saying anything that could be used by the defense."

Sally remained skeptical, "I've read stories about the Prosecutor's office and they appear to be tougher on the police than the criminals." She paused and lamented further, "And what's with the media in this town? Watching the local news, you'd never know this ever happened."

"Yeah, I hear you but let's give it a chance." She frowned skeptically. "But sure, I'll go with you." He tried to make light of the situation. "One thing is certain. You won't have any trouble identifying the perp after the way you messed up his face." She laughed nervously but at least seemed relieved to have Michael on board.

Days later, when Michael met Sally to head to City Hall, he didn't pick up on her edginess at first. He was too enamored by her cheery print dress that gave a vivacious look to her smallish but well-proportioned frame. Her perky walk added to his delight. Smiling broadly, he inquired, "Shall we take my car?"

"It's so close, let's hail a cab. The parking down there is such a pain."

Once inside the taxi together, her dour mood enveloped him. He tried to boost her morale, "Don't be so nervous, Sally. This will be a piece of cake."

It didn't help that the building looked like a medieval fortress. As they climbed the steps, Sally said glumly, "Welcome to the Bastille."

Michael tried to remain upbeat. He picked up on her French Revolution reference and quipped, "Don't worry, there are no guillotines inside." Sally didn't crack a smile. "Think of the good you're doing. You can help put this guy away for a long, long time. Plus, this could assist them in apprehending his three accomplices."

He couldn't have been more wrong if his name was Wrongy Wrongenstein. First off, it quickly became apparent that there'd be nothing routine about this visit when they were met by one of the City's attorneys who had the personality of a toadstool. She barely shook hands and remained stone-faced and completely inhospitable as she led them to a nearby meeting room while accompanied by a couple of stern-looking legal assistants. Sally whispered to Michael, "Should I have an attorney present?"

He whispered back, enjoying having his lips nearly touching her ears. "Let's be patient and give it a chance." Michael almost floated away on the enchanting fragrance of her perfume.

Any visions of seeing the perp in a lineup or confronting him behind bars or through thick plexiglass were obliterated as the door opened. The conference room, lined in rich mahogany, dripped with tradition and grandeur. Thus, it made the contrast that confronted them all the more shocking. They were astonished to see the barbaric thug who had accosted Sally dressed in a suit and lounging comfortably in a padded leather chair. He was flanked by his attorney and offered a defiant smirk when he saw us. Sally objected in a strident tone, "What's the meaning of this?"

The City's attorney tried to sound official, "There's nothing to worry about."

This only cranked up the concern in Sally's voice by several notches, "Why didn't you warn me you'd be putting me in harm's way?" The attorney looked nonplussed. "Where's the security in this place?"

Michael offered reassurance to Sally while glaring directly at the scar-faced perp. "Don't worry, I won't let this creep get near you." That threat wiped the smile right off of his face.

The City's attorney must have sensed she was losing control of the situation and waved in two security guards who were waiting just outside the door. "I can assure you that you're perfectly safe, Ms. Temple." Michael nodded at Sally and placed his hand on her shoulder. The City's attorney seized the opportunity, "Please take a seat."

They sat at the far end of the table and Michael placed himself between Sally and the creep. She challenged the City's attorney, "Do you mind telling me why we're here?"

Miss Personality responded in a dull monotone, "We just have a few questions for you, Ms. Temple. This won't take long." Sally whispered to Michael that she still felt she needed an attorney present but didn't formally object. "This is only a formality but, for the sake of full transparency, please be advised that this conversation is being recorded." Sally grabbed Michael's forearm and squeezed. He tried to calm her by placing his other hand over hers. "Thank you. Now, Ms. Temple, do you recall ever encountering Mr. Darnell-Wright?"

Sally was clearly agitated, "Oh, so that low-life, sorry excuse for a human being has a name?"

"Please, Ms. Temple, just answer the question."

Sally unloaded, "Encounter? If you mean, did he and three of his friends attack me and try to sexually ..."

The City's attorney rudely interrupted Sally in mid-sentence, "PLEASE, Ms. Temple! A simple yes or no will suffice."

"No, it will NOT SUFFICE!" The City's attorney raised her palm as if to put up a stop sign but Sally would have none of it. "That, that ANIMAL tried to sodomize me!" The City's Attorney tried to talk over her and Darnell-Wright's attorney shouted his objection at the same time. Sally drowned them both out, "I'm not sure what's going on here but I've given my statement to the police! Maybe you should read the report!"

The City's attorney tried to regain some semblance of order. "Yes, Ms. Temple, we've read the police report. Please, just bear with me. We're just trying to get the full story. Please help us with the details." There was a long pause before everyone calmed down. Then the City's attorney shifted gears and turned to the perp. "Mr. Darnell-Wright, is this the woman you allege attacked you?"

Sally went bonkers, "Attacked? Attacked? Have you ever heard of self-defense, lady? Do you want details? How about you swab under my fingernails? I'm sure you'll find his DNA under there. Yeah, I clawed the hell out of his face and I'd do it again in a New York minute! If I wouldn't have done that, he would have deposited some other kind of DNA in me!"

Darnell-Wright jumped out of his chair and lunged toward Sally. "Yeah, dat's da crazy," he caught himself before swearing, "dat ripped into my face!" He jumped to his feet and his attorney tried unsuccessfully to restrain him. The two City security guards were still behind Sally so, Wyatt stepped up and faced Darnell-Wright with his feet planted in a fighting stance and fists curled. The perp's memory must have served him well because he backed off immediately.

Pandemonium was averted when the two security guards grabbed Darnell-Wright and coerced him back into his seat. Nevertheless, Sally and Wyatt resisted when the City's attorney tried to coax them back to the table. Michael spoke on Sally's behalf, "This meeting is over. Any further discussions will need to be directed to Ms. Temple's attorney."

The City's attorney cautioned, "I must advise you that we're conducting an investigation into the matter at hand. The defendant, Mr. Darnell-

Wright, has accused Ms. Temple of an unprovoked attack triggered by racial animus. I strongly encourage you to cooperate."

This raised Michael Wyatt's ire, "We're finished." He led Sally out of the conference room and toward the exit.

The City's attorney followed them and shouted a final warning, "This could lead to charges of felony battery and possibly even a hate crime!"

It took quite a while for Sally to settle down. She was still visibly shaking as they rode back to work. After exiting the Uber, Michael suggested, "Let's go across the street for a cup of coffee before going back. You need a chance to gather yourself before returning to work."

By the look on her face, she appeared to stubbornly resist at first but then seemed to realize that Michael wasn't the enemy, "Good idea."

Michael was thrilled to have more personal time alone with Sally but, given the circumstances, used the opportunity to offer wise counsel. After recapping the lunacy they'd just experienced, he concluded, "You definitely need to hire an attorney."

"You're absolutely right but what about the cost? It's so unfair that I have to spend a bunch of money defending myself when I'm the victim!"

"I know but maybe there's a way to avoid going broke through legal fees." She gazed at him with watery but hopeful eyes. "There are a lot of conservative organizations out there that have been set up to help people just like you."

Her eyes lit up like blue candles, "Really?"

"Yeah, in fact, I've donated money to one. You've probably seen the guy who heads it up. He's on cable news all the time."

The mood turned around one-hundred-eighty degrees for the better and Sally raised her cup with a sublime look on her glowing face, "Cheers to you Michael Wyatt." As their mugs clinked, she added, "I guess I owe you my thanks once again." Michael started to raise his cup for a second toast but Sally stretched out her arm to stop him. "You must be my guardian angel." She stood and leaned across the table and planted another kiss on his forehead; this time firmly enough to leave red lipstick prints behind. Although the kiss was enough to send him to the moon, Michael may have been even more delighted by the way she carefully wiped away the smudge.

Michael had offered good advice that turned out to be true. He was happy for Sally when they agreed to take on her case gratis. He was even more ecstatic that, due to his involvement in the incident, they asked him to participate regularly in their briefings with Sally. As it turned out, Michael needed their legal assistance too. Darnell-Wright included him in his claims of being the victim of a racially-motivated, unprovoked attack.

It was an outrageously frivolous and fraudulent charge but, incredibly, the City backed Darnell-Wright. There was clear video evidence from the parking garage's security camera that should have made it a no-brainer. However, the City's attorneys tried to argue that the video footage was inadmissible in court. They would have been successful too if not for the dogged determination of Sally and Michael's legal team. With their deep pockets, they were able to convince the liberal judge who was ready to rule in favor of the City that they'd appeal to a higher court and, in the process, call for an investigation into the judge's malfeasance.

The judge wanted no part of a scenario that looked likely to land him personally in hot water. When he wavered, the City and Darnell-Wright had the monumental gall to seek an out-of-court settlement. With truth on their side and the steadfast, principled support of their legal team, Sally and Michael refused to cave. In a shameless, last-ditch attempt to wring some cash out of the actual victims, Darnell-Wright's team tried to apply pressure to their employer. Surprisingly in this day and age, the company refused to give into the attempted shakedown. It was the right thing to do morally but also made good business sense when Sally and Michael's lawyers quietly assured their employer that they'd face a much greater backlash if they were forced to expose them if they caved into blatant extortion.

It didn't seem like much of a victory when the City and Darnell-Wright dropped the case. There was nothing in the media about Sally and Michael being exonerated. Worst of all, Darnell-Wright and his partners in crime went scot free. If that wasn't bad enough, Sally and Michael had to endure salt being thrown into their wounds when Darnell-Wright went unpunished after hurling parting threats at them about how he wouldn't forget and that he'd get them someday. On that day though, Michael got the last laugh when he gave Darnell-Wright a sinister smile and pointed his hand at him as if it were a gun.

Chapter 4:

The next time they ran into each other at work, Sally asked, "What was that hand gesture you made toward that creep all about?"

Michael chuckled, "I Bronsoned him."

Her brow furrowed, "You what?"

"Don't tell me you've never heard of Charles Bronson."

Really curious now, Sally replied, "Nope."

Michael hesitated, not wanting to highlight their age difference but could tell he was in too deep to back out. "He was a big-time actor back in the 60s, 70s and 80s. Probably best known for *Death Wish*."

She teased, "Never heard of him. Before my time."

He attempted to shield himself with self-deprecating humor, "Ouch!" but she must have sensed she'd touched upon a real sore spot.

"Hey, I was only kidding."

He sounded self-conscious and fragile, "No big deal. It's a weird hobby of mine. I'm into classic flicks."

"No need to apologize. I love classic movies too." She almost said that her mom and dad had turned her onto the classics but stopped short realizing that it would only make matters worse.

"Really? But you've never heard of Charles Bronson?"

"Not my genre. I'm into girly stuff. You know, like *Gone with the Wind*. Or silly stuff like those old *Beach Party* movies."

"Oh, I love those too." He paused and offered a hopeful look. "How about this? What say we get together and watch *Death Wish*?

"I'd be delighted. When do you think they'll show it again on *TCM*?"

"I don't know but not to worry. I have all five *Death Wish* movies on DVD."

"Five?"

He laughed, "Don't worry. We can just watch the first one. That should be enough to explain my little hand gesture." The excitement over the prospect of spending some quality alone-time with Sally conquered any hesitancy about their age difference. "How about Friday evening at my place?"

"It's a date!"

His confidence wavered when he heard the word date. "Wow, a date. Are you sure you don't mind hanging out with an old geezer like me?"

Sally gave him a big boost, "Geezer? What are you forty, forty-five?"

He hesitated as if the words were stuck in his throat, "Fifty-two." She left him hanging when she didn't react, not even the slightest flinch. "How old are you, Sally, if you don't mind me asking?"

She pretended to be offended, "How dare you! That's not the kind of question you should ask a lady." Michael turned red and started sputtering but Sally busted out laughing before he could speak. "Relax, pops, I'm thirty-seven if you must know."

Michael was still too serious, "Fifteen years. That's a big gap."

Sally grabbed his bicep and squeezed, "Listen to me. You're in much better shape than most guys half your age. I don't know anyone as buff as you." He turned bright red. Sally turned the tables, "But, if you don't want to DATE someone as young as me, that's okay."

Relieved, his sense of humor finally kicked in, "I guess in the name of tolerance and inclusivity, I'll make an exception for you, squirt." She grinned in a way that took the mood from awkward and tense to completely relaxed. "Hey listen, since I live close by, how about if we go straight from work to dinner somewhere here downtown before heading to my place?"

"Sounds good. How about the Old Spaghetti Factory?"

"You don't mind the walk?"

"No, I can use the exercise. Plus, I love the Landing. Can we check out the riverboats and stroll underneath the Arch on the way back?"

"That sounds fantastic! What do you mean you could use the exercise? You look like you take pretty good care of yourself."

She twirled with delight, making her skirt flare out like a silken carousel. "I try to take advantage of the company gym now and then." She laughed as she pretended to strenuously hoist an imaginary dumbbell. Sally grabbed both sides of her skirt between her thumbs and forefingers daintily and offered Michael a reverent curtsy. "Thank you for noticing."

Michael beamed as he thought to himself, *Sally just keeps getting better. She works out, prefers casual over fancy dining, would rather walk than ride and digs old movies.* He blurted, "You're right up my alley, Sally." He frowned thinking, *why did I say something so corny?* "Sorry, that sounds so old-fashioned."

"Stop apologizing, Silly. I'm an old-fashioned girl at heart." To prove she wasn't just kidding, she laid a little trivia on him. "You just reminded me of an old song I like: *Sneakin' Sally Through the Alley* by Robert Palmer."

"You MUST be an old soul! I love that song too."

Friday couldn't roll around quickly enough for Michael. It didn't hurt that it was a beautiful evening. The Old Spaghetti Factory reeked of delightful history with shades of the old brick warehouse peeking out from behind the fine trappings adorning the walls and the richly sculpted, dark oaken furniture drawing attention away from the weathered floors. The food was simple but savory, enhanced by an earthy, deep red wine.

There was something magical about strolling from the restaurant over bumpy cobblestones that sloped steeply down to the river's edge. It required balance, care and, to Michael's delight, holding hands to maintain proper balance. With historic Eads Bridge above and a paddle wheeler anchored in the Mighty Mississippi below, it was easy to imagine the St. Louis riverfront of the late eighteenth century bustling with people transferring cargo from flatboats to wagons headed for the wild west.

Turning away from the water, the couple gazed upon the greatest monument to our nation's westward expansion: The Gateway Arch. It seemed to ascend even higher than its magnificent six-hundred-thirty-three-foot pinnacle since Sally and Michael were at the base of a steep, massive stone staircase stretching from Wharf Street to the Arch Grounds above. After the climb, they didn't stop to catch their breath but went directly to the right leg, pressed against it and looked straight up. The gleaming steel parabola soared impossibly upward toward the stars that were just beginning to pop out as dusk rolled toward night.

Sally exclaimed, "No matter how many times I've done this, it always amazes me." She looked at Michael with child-like wonder and then raised her head skyward again. "What must it have been like for the men who built the Arch?"

"Yeah, I love those old films they show in the museum below the Arch. I'm not afraid of heights but I don't think I could have done it."

"When I look up like this, I imagine myself hurtling from the top as if it were a giant playground slide."

"I know! Only I picture myself parachuting down on top of the Arch but then being unable to stop from plummeting down the side. Gives me the willies."

Sally pulled Michael down to the concrete so they could look up from a prone position, still holding hands, without craning their necks. It didn't matter that there were scads of other people around. They were off in another world. Sally said wistfully, "I wish we could go inside."

"Damn COVID."

"I love the way you can see the whole city from up top."

Michael sheepishly confessed, "I've lived here all my life and have never taken the tram to the top."

"What, are you kidding me? I thought you said you weren't afraid of heights. Are you claustrophobic?"

"No, nothing like that. I'm just impatient. I hate waiting in line." He chuckled softly, "I think it goes back to my first and only visit to Disney World. I was with my brother's kids and stood in line for over an hour to ride *It's a Small World*. It was hotter than all get out and the little guys were antsy and complaining the whole time. When we finally got in, what a letdown. It looked like a cheap carnival ride from the 1950s. And that incessant song! I can still hear it repeating in my head."

Sally laughed, "Will you go with me when it opens back up?"

Michael didn't hesitate, "It's a date!"

"Speaking of dates, let's keep this one moving. It's starting to get dark."

Michael couldn't help but think of their encounter with the four animals in the parking garage but didn't say anything about the mean streets of St. Louis. He didn't want to kill the mood and instead offered, "Isn't it fantastic what they've done with the Arch Grounds?"

"Magnificent!" She also didn't want to throw a wet blanket on their fun and squelched the thought; *too bad they haven't done as much for the statue of St. Louis IX over in Forest Park.*

Thankfully, their stroll to Michael's condo was uneventful. Once inside, Sally commented, "This is really nice. I love the view. We can see where we work, the stadium and Ball Park Village."

"Care for another glass of wine?"

"Are you trying to get me drunk?"

Michael tried not to blush, "Sorry, I didn't mean to come across the wrong way."

She shook her head playfully, "You need to chill, mister." Sally smiled at him disarmingly beneath bedroom eyes and he looked completely flummoxed. He remained awkwardly frozen as she advanced toward him slowly, like a jungle cat, and ran her fingers through his hair as she cupped the back of his head and pulled him in for a long, slow kiss. Then, much to his surprise, she turned on her heels and pranced to the couch. She sat down and patted the cushion next to her and blithely said, "Pop in the movie."

Confused, Michael did a double-take and asked, "What was that all about?"

Without batting an eyelash, she calmly replied, "I told you that you needed to chill." Behind a Cheshire grin, she added, "Don't you feel more relaxed now that we've gotten that out of the way?" Speechless, Michael shook his head and muttered something unintelligible as he headed toward the Blue Ray player.

Michael sat close to Sally and hit play. The relaxing atmosphere soon evaporated when, early on, *Paul Kersey's* wife and daughter were accosted in their New York apartment by a group of vicious thugs that were all too reminiscent of the four brutes that attacked Sally in the parking garage. Her body tensed as the on-screen hyenas brutally beat *Kersey's* wife to death and ravaged his daughter so badly it hurled her into a state of catatonic shock. Michael didn't interrupt he movie by trying to offer soothing words but instead simply put his strong arm around Sally.

Although Sally seemed really engrossed in the movie, she curled up like a purring kitten under the shelter of Michael's arm. They not only relaxed again but grew very comfortable with each other's touch even though there was no canoodling. Sally interrupted their serenity when she suddenly demanded, "Hit pause!" Michael didn't question her but rather grabbed the remote and followed orders. He looked at her for affirmation. "No, wait. Go back." He did as she had asked and hit rewind with only one arrow. "There, stop!"

When he looked at the screen, he knew immediately what had caught her eye. Michael squeezed her tightly and pressed his cheek against hers without kissing Sally, "Bravo! You're very observant!" On the screen, Charles Bronson as *Paul Kersey* flashed a devilish grin as he stared down a depraved thug and pretended to shoot him with an imaginary gun.

She stated matter-of-factly, "Now I see."

"Do you want to watch something else now that our mission has been accomplished?"

"Heck no! I want to see the whole thing; every last minute."

Michael grinned, "Yeah, I've noticed how you've been cheering every time Kersey takes down another creep."

"I can't help it. He reminds me of my real-life hero." Before embarrassment could set in, Sally leaned in hard, embraced Michael tightly and laid a kiss on him that could have curled his hair.

He didn't want to stop but something told him to put the brakes on. Almost eye-to-eye, Michael offered this lame excuse, "We should get back to the movie, don't you think?"

Sally appeared to be sincerely perplexed, "Did I do something wrong?"

"No, no, that was the greatest kiss of." He caught himself to ward off hyperbole.

Sally, still close enough that Michael could feel her breath, looked at him doe-eyed, "Well, there's more where that came from, mister."

"I'm so sorry."

"Sorry for what, Michael?"

There was a long pregnant pause because Sally really needed to know. Michael struggled to come up with an excuse and finally settled for the bare truth. "I don't know quite how to say this. It's going to sound way too forward but it's the way I feel." Sally remained silent but urged him on with limpid blue, deeply sympathetic eyes. "I can't explain it. We've only known each other for such a short time but." She didn't budge and her magnetic eyes continued to draw the truth out of him. "Darn it! I think there's something very special about you!" He sounded flustered, almost defensive. "There's something between us." He exhaled loudly. "I don't want to mess things up by going too far too fast."

Sally gazed at him with such sweet, innocent eyes that it calmed his racing heart as if a roaring car engine had been shifted into neutral. Without a word, she moved away just enough to end their embrace but she remained at his side. She took his hand and placed it on her thigh and laid hers on top of his. As she rested her head on Michael's shoulder, she conferred, "Let's finish our movie." Before he could press play, she lifted her head and playfully challenged him, "You don't think I'm some kind of floozy, do you?"

Now, Michael had the confidence to fire back, "Not as long as you don't think I'm a prude," She smiled softly and cuddled her head back into his shoulder. It didn't last for long because, as Michael well knew, the credits were about to roll.

When the movie ended, Sally threw herself at Michael and exclaimed, "Okay, now let's get back to making out!" She chortled at the panicked look on his face and quickly let him off the hook. "I'm kidding, silly!" He heaved a sigh of relief. "I'm with you. Let's take it slow and get to know each other."

"Alright, Sally. What do you suggest?"

"How about twenty questions?"

"I'm game. Ladies first."

Sally massaged her chin and appeared to put a lot of thought into the process. "How come you're working as a security guard?" Michael looked ashamed and embarrassed. "I'm sorry. I didn't mean to offend you. There's nothing wrong with being a security guard. I mean, look at what you did for me. You saved my life." This seemed to give Michael a bit of a boost. "It's just that you seem to be a really smart guy; much smarter than a lot of the bosses where we work."

"I used to be a boss," he put air quotes around the last word. "I had quite a few people working for me, lots of responsibility and made a bunch of money."

"What happened?"

"I opened my big mouth." Sally had a tell-me-more look on her face. "It's a long story but let me sum it up for you. After years of having diversity and inclusiveness shoved down my throat, I couldn't take some young punk preaching morality to me and telling me how to think."

"Go on."

"I knew I'd be fired but, after careful consideration, I basically told the boss to take a flying leap at a rolling donut."

"Wow!"

"Thankfully, I'd saved well for my retirement but needed to bridge the gap until I could get my hands on my pension."

"And you decided to take a job as a security guard?" He explained his rationale and circumstances. She echoed his earlier sentiments, "Makes sense. Damn virus!" She paused to reflect on her own situation, "You think you had it bad? How would you like to be in HR? We have to peddle that junk every day."

Michael placed his hands together as if in prayer and bowed to concede the point to her before moving on. "Okay then, I guess it's my turn." Michael didn't need to ponder for long. "How is it that a knockout like you isn't married?"

"I was married once."

"Divorced?"

"No, my husband died."

Michael gulped, "Oh Sally, I'm so sorry. What happened?"

"Michael – yeah that was his name, by chance. Michael and I got married in 2007 when we were both twenty-four; very young by today's standards. We each had earned college degrees and the future looked bright." She appeared lost in thought like her mind was time-traveling. "Michael was old-school too; a real patriot. Back then, terrorism and 9/11 were still top of mind. The war in the Middle East wasn't going so well and many people thought we should leave Iraq. I'm sure you remember when President Bush doubled down with his surge and sent more troops to fight in Iraq and then Afghanistan."

"Yes, I remember it well."

"Michael didn't hesitate. He immediately approached me about him joining the Marines. I gave him my full support." Her eyes grew moist as if she still harbored some personal guilt over his death. "He went all in, Semper Fi and the whole thing." She dipped her head to the side, still expressing some indecision. "Would I have been so supportive if I'd known then that he would sign up for multiple tours of duty over the next six years? I don't know."

She shrugged, "This I do know. We both sacrificed a lot for our country. I spent countless lonely hours missing him terribly. Any plans for starting a family were kept on hold. With nothing else to maintain my sanity, I threw myself into my work and career."

"Was he killed in combat?"

"No, that's the ironic thing. He fought in numerous bloody battles and lost many brothers in arms. Many others came home maimed for life. Not Michael, though. After six long years, he came home without a scratch." Sadness overcame Sally and then a flash of anger as she recounted their tragic marriage. "Most guys with a college degree in finance and accounting would have gone into business but not altruistic Michael. He wanted to continue to serve in a different capacity." She wiped away a tear. "So, what did he do?" Sally thew up her hands in frustration. "He went to the academy and became a police officer."

"What jurisdiction?"

"He was a County cop. Just our luck. He was in his first year on the force when that crap in Ferguson blew up." She had to stop to control her churning emotions.

"Sally, you don't need to go on. This was a bad idea."

"No, I want to get this off of my chest. You need to know." Michael nodded reverently. "I think life after the Marine Corps was worse than when I had to wonder if he'd make it home from Iraq and Afghanistan. At least when he was over there, the nightly news wasn't constantly reminding me of the danger he faced. When he put on the badge, I was on pins and needles every night listening for the key to turn the lock in the door." She lowered her head momentarily and then raised it defiantly. "Then he got called to Ferguson."

Sally paused as if to draw on a hidden reserve of strength and determination. "I laid awake every night, all alone. How could I sleep with all those visions of burning, looting and insane violence in my brain?" Indignant rage flared in her eyes. "All because of some overgrown, drugged-up thug who stole from a convenience store and then tried to kill a cop. Hands up, don't shoot, my ass!"

It took a while for her to regain her composure. "One night, Michael didn't come home. Instead, two other officers knocked at my door with the bad news." She glared at Michael through red-rimmed eyes, "And the worst part? They never caught the guy. Some complete coward took a random potshot from the shadows at a group of officers. Michael was the one who took the bullet. Right through his heart."

Michael swallowed her up in his arms and swayed slowly, side-to-side, until she seemed at peace. "Hey, how about we pop in another movie? Are you up for *Beach Blanket Bingo* or *Muscle Beach Party?*"

Sally straightened up and grabbed Michael by the shoulders, "No way, mister! I'm not letting you off the hook. It's my turn again."

"Whatever you say, boss."

They moved over to the kitchen table. "Turnabout is fair play. How is it that a stud like you is free and single?" She joked, "You are single, aren't you? You aren't one of those creeps leading dual lives, are you?"

"Sorry, there's nothing that exciting in my life."

"What gives then?" When Michael hesitated while contemplating how to explain his situation, Sally must have thought she'd made a terrible mistake. "Oh Michael, I'm sorry if this is off limits. I can ask a different question."

"Heaven's no. I was just gathering my thoughts. We're not so different. I was married too." Sally looked shocked as if she'd opened a can of worms. Michael laughed softly, "No, she didn't die. The witch divorced me."

Sally exhaled and looked relieved, "Oh, that's good. No, wait. I didn't mean it that way. I was just glad that she didn't die."

Michael tried to make light of the situation, "Oh, she's dead alright. At least she's dead to me."

She slapped him playfully on the arm, "Oh, you!" He smiled back at her and she followed with, "Seriously, though. What happened?"

"I guess I should blame myself. Simply put, I made a bad choice." Sally remained mum, not willing to settle for such a threadbare explanation. "Looking back, I don't think she ever really loved me, at least not the way it's supposed to work in a Christian marriage." Sally raised her eyebrows. He chuckled, "Get your mind out of the gutter, Sally. She wasn't unfaithful in that way as far as I could tell. We just didn't share the kind of bond necessary to make it through rough times. You know, the kind of self-sacrificing love that conquers all." Sally confirmed she was tracking with him through a simple nod. "I was a good provider and all but I think the kicker was when she found out I couldn't give her children."

"Oh, I see."

"Do you want to have kids, Sally?"

"I'm not a spring chicken anymore."

"C'mon, Sally. Lots of women are having children in their late thirties these days."

"Not me. That parade has passed me by." Michael squinted, perplexed. "Even if I still wanted children, ovarian cancer took that off the table for me."

"I'm so sorry."

"No need to be sorry, Michael. Apparently, God has other plans for me."

"We could always adopt." Michael's face flushed red as he realized his tongue had gotten ahead of his brain, "Sorry, I got carried away. We're supposed to be taking this slowly."

"No problemo, Miguel. Your turn."

"Okay Sallito. Hmmmm, you mentioned God. I'm assuming you're a Christian?" Sally's countenance fell and she seemed very hesitant to answer. "Oh, oh, should we declare politics and religion off limits?"

"No, no. If we're going to do this, we might as well get down into the weeds." She gathered herself. "You see, Michael. I really like you and, I guess, I was worried this could be a deal breaker. But, if so, better to find out up front rather than later."

"Agreed."

"By the way, just as an aside, would you wear a red MAGA hat?" Michael hooted like Nature Boy Ric Flair and shoved both thumbs up in the air. Sally conferred by mimicking Macho Man Randy Savage, "Ohhhh yeeeaaaahhh! Now that the easy part is behind us, let's get to the tough stuff."

Michael snickered, "Is this where you break out your pentagram and goat's head?"

Sally grew serious, "To the contrary, I'm old-school when it comes to religion too. I'm a Lutheran. And I don't mean one of those newfangled ones. I'm talking died-in-the-wool Missouri Synod. A real Bible thumper." She shrugged, palms up and added, "Go ahead, run for the hills."

Michael guffawed uncontrollably. He laughed so hard and long that he almost cried. Sally's smile flatlined and then the corners of her mouth bowed steeply downward in deep disappointment. It was like an ax had fallen on Michael's cackling when he realized his faux pas had greatly offended her. "Sally, forgive me. I wasn't laughing at you." She stared with the sad eyes of a little girl waiting for her daddy to apologize for falsely accusing her. "I was laughing at the incredible coincidence." Her face became a question mark. "I couldn't believe my good luck!"

"What are you talking about?"

"I'm Lutheran too. LC-MS all the way."

"No way!"

"Sola Scriptura, Formula of Concord and the whole ball of wax." Her jaw dropped at this good news. "I couldn't stop laughing at the way you thought your faith would be a deal breaker." She hugged him tightly for the longest time. "Hallelujah and amen!"

"Where do you worship, Michael?"

"I go all the way up to North County to Trinity Lutheran. It's one of the few times I use my car these days."

"Why there? Is that where you were brought up?"

"No, it's just the most solid church I've been able to find. They practice close communion and stick to God's word no matter how unpopular it might be in today's world." He studied Sally's face for any hint of disapproval and found none. "How about you?"

"I'm pretty much in the same boat except that I headed to South County to get the pure gospel." She bubbled over with enthusiasm, "Hey, I've got an idea! How about if we worship together and compare notes?"

"Sure, we can go to your church this week and worship with my congregation next."

Sally extended her hand to shake on it, "It's a deal." With that settled, a mischievous look crept over her face. "What now? Wanna make out?" She poked him in the ribs and snorted, "Just kidding, Pops! Let's watch *Beach Party*."

Chapter 5:

Their experiment in congregational comparisons went extremely well. Both churches proved very confessional and this served to highlight the good judgment exhibited by both Michael and Sally. It provided a rock-solid foundation on which to build their relationship. However, this left them with a bit of a dilemma. Consequently, they quickly resolved to continue worshipping together while attending each of their churches on alternating Sundays. They soon became an item among the members of both congregations.

As their relationship blossomed, Michael took a hiatus from his nightly vigils along the mean streets of St. Louis. He and Sally couldn't get enough of each other and their almost constant companionship filled the void he'd felt before. They were lost in their own little paradise except for one nagging problem. The world around them didn't stop turning or churning. There was no escaping the cloying depression of the draconian measures that had been deployed by St. Louis City and County, supposedly, to combat the virus. As weeks turned into months, it became apparent that it was about politics more than science.

To make matters worse, cynical, power-hungry politicians added a lethal ingredient to the evil elixir they'd concocted to sow fear and panic. After all, it was an election year. As one of their Democrat cohorts once famously said, they weren't about to let a good crisis go to waste. So, instead of downplaying the virus, they added fuel to the fire. They highjacked the social justice movement to unleash violence and mayhem into the streets of cities and towns all across America. It created an atmosphere of lawlessness that caused crime to spike in most major metropolitan areas. St. Louis was no exception.

At least Sally and Michael could commiserate with one another. This provided them with a healthy outlet for the fears and frustrations they shared with many people across the country. Still, the daily barrage of images spewing from cable news was unsettling. The most unbelievable thing was the way that liberal mayors and governors were not only allowing anarchy to take over their streets but, in some cases, actually encouraged it.

This discussion was typical of the conversations Michael and Sally shared on a regular basis. It occurred over dinner at a restaurant in bordering St. Charles County where masks weren't required. Sally observed, "Isn't it amazing? Just by crossing the Missouri River, we've escaped the virus."

"Yes, this Corona thing is the most intelligent virus ever known to mankind. It understands geography. The virus can sense that it's not allowed to cross the river into St. Charles."

"You're so right, Michael. Even within St. Louis County it knows to only attack people without a mask in the doorway to a restaurant. It doesn't spread inside to tables where people are eating and drinking without their masks. Even though it's supposedly airborne, it can't circulate anywhere but the restaurant lobby."

Michael snickered, "The most amazing thing of all is how it knows to attack people in church or a sporting event but can't touch people when they're elbow-to-elbow at a riot."

Sally corrected him, "Riot? Didn't you mean peaceful protest?"

"Yes, please excuse me for misspeaking."

"That's better. I just hope a group of peaceful protesters from BLM don't beat the hell out of us for eating dinner here."

"That's not likely to happen here in St. Charles. But just in case, I'm ready," he tapped the Glock strapped to his mid-section under his Polo.

Sally grew serious, "Would you really use it?"

"In a heartbeat. I mean, if someone actually tried to force us to say something we didn't want to say or if they tried to hurt you."

"What about turning the other cheek?"

"Christ never said we shouldn't defend ourselves. Self-defense is the law of the land."

"Shouldn't we listen to God before government, though? You know, give unto Caesar what is Caesar's and to God what is God's."

"God gave us government, according to Romans 13, for the purpose of promoting good and curbing evil. Thankfully, this country and our Constitution were founded on God's word in the Bible. Our rights, as listed therein, were granted not by the government but attributed to God Himself. We have the right to life, liberty and the pursuit of happiness. We can worship and speak our minds freely. Yes, we need to worship and serve God above all else but we should live according to the law and respect government for its God-given purpose. That's part of the Fourth Commandment. It's not just about parental authority."

"I'm not disagreeing with you, Michael. I just wanted to get your take on this."

"Playing devil's advocate, eh?" he chortled.

"Yeah, the devil made me do it. Very funny, mister!"

"Just kidding but I get it, Sally. I don't want to hurt anyone either but I think we both understand there's a line that can't be crossed. You've read BLM's manifesto, right?" She nodded. "They're not only anti-capitalist and anti-American but diametrically opposed to Jesus Christ and His followers." She nodded her consent again. "What would you do if they demanded that you denounce your faith in Jesus Christ?"

"You're right, Michael. There comes a time when we can't turn the other cheek. There comes a time when we must take a stand." She paused before adding, "Jesus said if you deny me before men, I'll deny you before my Father in heaven."

"Bravo!" Satisfied, Michael tried to switch gears. "I hope we're never caught in a situation where I'd have to use my gun." He smiled and raised his glass of Budweiser to toast with Sally. "Isn't it nice to be over here in St. Charles, gazing out at the river?"

"I love watching it roll by. It's like we're on another planet. Right over there, across the Muddy Missouri, it's a world apart. But here, it just feels different with virtually no masks and all that other stuff."

Michael agreed, "Yep, I love seeing the friendly smiles on people's faces."

After they finished their dinner and took a stroll down by the banks of the Missouri, Sally lamented, "Sorry Hon but I have an early meeting tomorrow. I guess we should head back."

Michael added, tongue-in-cheek, "Goodbye St. Charles. Hello cruel world."

Although fifty-two, Michael could have been a teenager infected with spring fever. Despite seeing each other almost every day, he couldn't get enough of Sally. They'd had dinner the night before but he was anxious by the time her meeting was finally over so they could grab a sandwich together in the company cafeteria. "I missed you," wasn't met with her radiant smile and normal reply of *I miss you more*. "What's the matter, babe?"

She tried to shrug it off, "Oh, nothing. It's just been a hectic morning."

"How could one of those boring HR meetings you're always telling me about be hectic?" She didn't giggle when he nudged her playfully. "Now I know something's wrong."

"I'd rather not talk about it. Can we change the subject?"

"Sally, you're not like this. Something must really be bothering you." He reached across the table and put his hand gently over hers. "You might as well get it off your chest. You'll feel better."

He waited patiently while patting her hand. She spoke in a hushed tone, "Something happened last night after you dropped me off."

Michael withdrew his hand and sat bolt upright, "What? Did somebody hurt you?"

"No, nothing physical," she reached over and took Michael's hand to reassure him. Then she produced an envelope containing a piece of folded paper. "This was wedged in my front door when I got home."

He unfolded it slowly as if there might be a deadly substance inside. The barely legible note simply read, "I told you I'd find you and get you." It ended with a misogynistic, racial epithet.

Michael's face looked like a pressure-cooker about to explode. Sally tried to calm him down, "He's just trying to scare me."

Michael was deadly serious, "Who are you trying to kid? You know what this guy is like. He's a vicious thug who wants to do more than just scare you." Hearing the frightening truth, Sally couldn't hold back her tears. This forced Michael to adopt a gentler tone in spite of his anger. "Don't worry, Sally. We're going right to the police to report this guy. Then, we're going to look into a restraining order against Mr. Darnell-Wright."

Sally was a realist, "Do you really think that will stop this maniac?" Michael attempted a rebuttal but stopped in mid-sentence since he knew better. "I know you mean well but let's face the facts. This guy has absolutely no respect for the law. A restraining order wouldn't slow him down for a second." Michael nodded grudgingly. "As for the police, they can't even protect themselves. They've been hung out to dry by the liberal mayors and governors. How many have been killed or seriously injured already this year?"

"Sadly, you're right. Here in our own town, that retired police captain was gunned down recently just for trying to stop the looters. And he was black! I guess ALL black lives don't matter." Michael paused and caught himself when he realized his venting wasn't helping Sally. "We still need to follow proper protocol with the police to put things on record." Sally sighed as if defeated. "But we won't stop there. We're going to be proactive rather than reactive."

"What do you mean, Michael?"

"You need around-the-clock protection."

Sally scoffed, "What are you going to do, Mr. Money Bags, hire an armed body guard?"

Michael puffed out his chest and patted his service revolver, "It won't cost you a penny."

"I know you'll protect me but you won't always be around."

He offered a stern smile brimming with confidence, "That's where you're wrong, sweetie."

"Huh?"

"You're moving in with me."

"What? You know we can't do that!"

Michael huffed, "I don't mean LIVING TOGETHER like friends with benefits."

Sally was equally animated, "Well, as a self-proclaimed, old-school Lutheran, I'm glad to hear you're not willing to abandon your principles." She paused to think and a sly smile crept over her face. "Michael, are you proposing to me?"

This chipped away at his confidence and he sounded flustered, "C'mon Sally, you said you wanted to take things slow." She feigned being crushed. He countered with, "If that's what it would take to keep you safe, then sure, I'd drop to one knee and offer you a ring."

"Aw, that's sooooooo sweet, Michael. But I'm not fishing for a proposal."

He pretended to wipe the sweat from his brow, "Phew!"

She laughed at his tomfoolery, "Very funny!" but pivoted to a serious tone. "So, then what did you have in mind if not tying the knot?"

"You can move into my place, with me as your bodyguard." She shot a skeptical glance at him. "No, really. You can sleep in the extra bedroom. No funny business. I promise."

Sally seemed to warm up to the idea, "Just until the threat passes? Strictly business?"

"Strictly business. I cross my heart."

"Why your place instead of mine?"

"Because he knows where you live."

Sally pressed him, "You don't think he'll be able to figure out where you live?"

"Yeah but my place is much closer to work and the condo complex is equipped with multiple security cameras. Also, I can escort you to and from work." He could tell she was close to agreeing. "Besides, my place has a much better view."

"I can't argue with that."

"Then it's settled. Right after work, we'll go and pack up your clothes and essentials."

As promised, Michael followed through on notifying the police but was stymied in seeking a restraining order. The judge, with input from the Prosecutor's office, ruled that there wasn't enough hard evidence to link the anonymous threat to Darnell-Wright. Michael figured that, in truth, it wouldn't have mattered if the thug had signed his name in blood. Although frustrated by the system, Michael could take heart that he'd at least made them file a record of his request for future reference.

Once Sally was settled in, Michael teased her about how a tornado had torn through his freakishly neat bachelor pad. "I guess I'll have to set up shop in the powder room. The master bathroom looks like something from an episode of *Hoarders*."

"Don't be so dramatic." Her mock frown turned into a gleeful grin, "You can tolerate a little clutter for this, can't you?" she framed her face with both of her index fingers. Sally feigned a chill, "You wouldn't want to see me without my face paint, trust me."

"Heavens no!" he shot back. "Can you wait until I've gone to bed to take it off?"

Things got interesting when they changed out of their work clothes to watch some TV together before bedtime. Michael donned a t-shirt and gym shorts. Sally selected her most modest PJs but still went sleeveless and shorty. After all, it was June and not January. To counter the distraction, Michael offered her a light linen comforter. She invited him to share it but playfully warned him before they cuddled up, "Remember, strictly business. Now, pay attention to the movie."

Things grew a little weird when they kissed before heading to their separate bedrooms. Michael took pains to hold up his end of the bargain by leaning forward to keep some distance between their bodies when he pecked her on the lips. No matter how hard he tried, Michael couldn't fall asleep. His mind kept wandering to Sally and how she was only a few feet away in the other bedroom. Eventually, his eyelids grew heavy.

Sally was tickled by Michael's gallantry and the way he was bound by his vow to maintain her honor. Yet, she couldn't help but be amused by his awkwardness in remaining chaste. It reminded her of one of those romantic farces starring Doris Day and Rock Hudson. Her playfulness wouldn't let her pass up an opportunity to gig him a little. She tip-toed into his bedroom and slid under the covers with him. This startled the drowsy dozer, "Sally, what are you doing?"

She clung to him tightly as if frightened, "I thought I heard a noise," she whispered frantically.

He lurched to get out of bed and check for prowlers but she grasped him even firmer and pleaded, "Don't leave me alone here!"

He bought into her ruse hook, line and sinker, "I'm not going to leave you. I just want to check out the condo and make sure everything is okay." She reluctantly and slowly released her grip. "Stay right there. This will only take a minute." He opened the nightstand and took out his Glock.

"Michael, wait."

"Shhhhh!" He glided silently across the bedroom and out into the main living area. All was quiet until there was a loud thud followed by unintelligible cursing and some commotion as a metal object clanged across the kitchen counter and something made of glass shattered on the floor. Michael continued to mutter words that Sally thankfully couldn't make out. A switch clicked and faint light filtered in from the kitchen.

When Michael returned to the bedroom, he had the Glock in his left hand and was rubbing his thigh with his right. "You must have been dreaming. We're the only one's making noise in the whole complex."

Sally looked sheepish with the covers pulled up around her shoulders and a look of embarrassment and regret on her face. "Michael, I'm so sorry. I was only kidding. It was a joke." He pretended to be close to blowing his top. "I was only teasing." Michael continued to glower as he approached her menacingly. "I couldn't stop thinking about your chivalry. My naughty side wanted to put your self-control to the test." She shrugged apologetically, almost pathetically, "Sorry."

By this time, Michael was next to the bed, towering over her. He lunged at Sally so convincingly that she gasped. Then he grabbed her sides and tickled her ribs until she begged for mercy, "Please stop! No more! I surrender!"

Michael ceased and calmly pulled back the covers and waved Sally toward her own room, "One good turn deserves another," he smirked.

"Oh you!" she huffed. Then sweetly, "I guess I deserved that."

Not finished yet, Michael needled her one more time, "Excuse me but could you turn out the light on your way out? You're scaring me without your makeup." Sally turned on her heels and rushed him. Before he could defend himself, she raised a pillow and began pummeling him until he grabbed her and pulled her in close. Then he gently brushed her hair back, embraced her face between his palms and kissed her passionately. "Who needs makeup? You, my dear, look better than ever. Au natural." Sally nearly floated on air as she returned to her own bedroom.

Some of the awkwardness faded as they fell into a routine over the next couple of weeks. However, this only added to the difficulty of maintaining self-control. One Saturday afternoon, Michael suggested, "We need to get out of this place for a while. Wanna take a long walk around Creve Coeur Lake?"

"I'd love to get out of the city for a while."

"Afterward, how about dinner at the Lake House?"

"That sounds fantastic. Can we share one of those giant Long Island Teas?"

"Super!"

Their getaway helped to take their minds off of everything. While it offered a new perspective, one thing didn't change. They adored each other and relished every moment together. Michael captured the feeling perfectly as they pulled away from the restaurant, "Whoever said that absence makes the heart grow fonder was crazy."

Sally concurred by thumbing through her iPod song list until she found *Can't Get Enough* by Bad Company. When the tune was over, Michael affected his deepest baritone and started crooning Barry White's, *Can't Get Enough of Your Love.*

Sally clapped and laughed before her practical side took over. "I've been thinking. Isn't it about time that I moved back into my own place?"

"It's only been three weeks."

"But there hasn't been any sign of trouble. Maybe Darnell-Wright and his pals have moved on."

"I don't know. Let me think about it." Michael didn't have to think for long. Shock overtook them both as they pulled up to Sally's house. Two windows were badly shattered and a raised black fist was spray-painted on the front door. It was a somber ride back to Michael's condo downtown. He soberly summed up the situation thusly, "You won't be moving back home anytime soon."

Back at Michael's place, they tried to maintain their normal routine but there seemed to be a dark cloud over them. Even campy horror host *Svengoolie* couldn't cut through the malaise with *Abbott and Costello Meet Frankenstein.* When comedy failed, Sally tried to wrest them from the doldrums with logic. "We can't go on like this forever, Michael. Maybe I should sell my house and buy a condo down here."

"That wouldn't make any sense. What a waste of money." It wasn't like Michael to be rude, especially to Sally, but he turned and went into his bedroom. She didn't want to look like a drama queen so, Sally stayed put on the couch and didn't say a word but couldn't hold back some silent tears. She wiped them away when he came back unexpectedly but couldn't hide the redness they'd left behind. "I'm sorry, honey, I didn't mean to upset you."

"It's all right. Don't pay any attention to silly me. I'm usually not so sensitive."

"What I said was true. But I have a better solution." Sally tried to muster some optimism while gazing up at him. "Please, come stand over here by me."

She stood up and approached him apprehensively. "My word, so formal!"

Before she knew what hit her, Michael dropped to one knee and stretched out his right hand revealing a small felt box. She had to lock her knees to keep them from buckling. He placed his left hand on Sally's waist to steady her. Once she'd regained her equilibrium, Michael flipped open the case to reveal a stunningly large, dazzlingly brilliant stone. "Sally Elaine Temple, will you marry me?"

"That's your solution?" He didn't move. She was at a loss for words.

"I'm waiting, dear."

She reflexively tried to fight the madness, "Hold on! Are you proposing marriage or a security protocol?" Sally didn't give him a chance to respond. "I appreciate the sentiment but this is no basis for a marriage." Michael remained patient, immobile. "This is crazy. Get up from there." He didn't budge so; she made a desperation play. "How much did you pay for that rock? It must have cost a fortune." No reply. "This is what you call taking it slowly?"

Michael remained on one knee, "Think for a minute. I didn't do this on impulse. I purchased the ring before we ever saw the horrible graffiti that vandal painted on your door. My mind was basically made up some time ago."

"But this is so sudden."

"I know we said we were going to take things slowly but I learned something very important as a business executive. Once you've reached a conclusion, you've got to strike while the iron is hot." His eyes bored in on hers, directly and deeply. "This has nothing to do with Darnell-Wright and those other thugs. Sally, you're the one for me. I know it deep down in my heart. Will you make me the happiest man in the world and marry me?"

"But weddings take planning and time."

"I'm starting to get the idea that you don't feel the same way about me."

"Oh, but I do!"

"Then why all the excuses?"

She stared up into the heavens and then peered down into Michael's hopeful eyes, "Yes, yes, yes – I'll marry you Michael Wyatt! I love you! I love you so much!"

He stood up and they embraced in a long, tender kiss. They lingered in complete bliss until Sally finally drew back to arms-length but remained emotionally locked-in with dreamy, lovesick eyes. Suddenly, panic set in as she wondered aloud, "When, where? There's so much to do!"

"Whoa there! Slow down and take a deep breath." He offered a sober look. "This isn't the first rodeo for either one of us. We don't need a big, fancy wedding. We can have a church wedding with a small gathering of close friends and family afterward. No need for a lot of planning. We can do this right away. Besides, you and I both know the key to a successful marriage."

She finished the thought for him, "Keeping Christ in the center."

Michael hugged Sally as they twisted back and forth like they were on a swivel. "We can get married right away and won't have to go into hock."

She jested, "If you're so concerned about debt, why did you buy the Hope Diamond?" He laughed casually but she was somewhat serious. "Really, how much did it set you back?"

"Don't you worry, Sally. You're worth every penny and then some."

Chapter 6:

Everything went smoothly and within three
weeks the happy couple was honeymooning in
Gulf Shores, Alabama. It seemed easy to escape
the madness while they were away. Although a
tourist town, it wasn't jam-packed with wall-to-
wall people like a lot of other beach destinations.
The laid-back atmosphere was complimented by
sparkling white sand and alluring aqua swells that
lapped leisurely against the shoreline with the
rhythmic comfort of a masseuse's hands. Lolling
in the sun's soothing rays and being caressed by
gentle breezes drifting off the Gulf left them in a
dreamlike state of mind. The toughest decision
they faced was whether to stroll over to the Sea 'n
Suds or grab lunch at the resort's snack shack.

It helped that they'd made a pact to never turn
on the news the entire week. However, despite
the blissful ignorance of their protective bubble,
life went on elsewhere. Things hadn't changed in
the real world. In fact, the crime, violence and
rancor only seemed to worsen as election-year
insanity ratcheted up to unprecedented levels.
Death tolls from gangland shootings and
ambushes staged against the police skyrocketed
while anarchists demanded that law enforcement
be defunded. The folks in depressed communities
who had to live with the violence wanted a

greater police presence but their voices weren't heard. That's because feverish progressive politicians kept pounding the social justice drums to appease and incite the loony left.

When some towns like Seattle had to say enough is enough and clamp down, most others declined the help offered by the Feds. Even when state or federal law enforcement got involved, local prosecutors practiced catch-and-release policies that put dangerous felons back on the street within hours. There were revolving doors on court buildings that spit out criminals faster than the cops could arrest them. Yet, at the same time, liberal Dems running major cities and counties kept law-abiding citizens under virtual house arrest with their politically-driven COVID-19 lockdowns.

This had a chilling effect on the morale of law enforcement. Police officers began retiring at an alarming rate and it was nearly impossible to recruit replacements since standing behind a badge literally entailed putting one's life at risk every single day. As the esprit de corps of law enforcement cratered, criminals were emboldened. The fecklessness of local liberal leaders gave a second wind to hoodlums, crooks and thugs.

The cops knew their mayors and some governors didn't have their backs. Proactive policing often led to heat coming down on the cops rather than the criminals. If someone threatened a cop with a knife or gun and the officer used deadly force to stop them, the cop would be fired and arrested while the thug was lionized by the media and sports figures. Rioters, fired up by media narratives, seized every opportunity to stoke the flames of anarchy. The rule of law was effectively placed on a ventilator. Due process was taken off life support.

The shifting tide toward lawlessness wasn't lost on Darnell-Wright and his sadistic sycophants. They didn't have to lurk in the shadows satisfying their violent urges through unremunerative hobbies like the knockout game. The four thugs could ply their pernicious trade right out in the open while posing as peaceful protesters. The heck with running from the cops. They could get right up in their faces while screaming obscenities with nary a worry over reprisals from the pigs, as they called them. Darnell-Wright and company expanded their brutal business to include profitable pursuits such as looting, robbery and extortion. They also became mercenaries by hooking up with powerbrokers that actually paid them to riot in the streets.

Even with all of their newfound, lucrative outlets for their sociopathic tendencies, they weren't distracted from their vengeful lusts in the least. Darnell-Wright remained committed to settling the score with Sally and Michael. It was a matter of street cred. In order to burnish his own surly reputation as a young tough on the rise, he had to make them pay. The former knockout king had to lay down the law to discourage anyone from ever crossing him. If nothing else, the lowlife creep was ambitious. Making an example out of Sally would show that he was going places.

One couldn't blame Michael and Sally for letting their guard down a bit. Being home and back at work couldn't dampen the glow surrounding them. It was as if they'd brought a little bit of the beach back from Gulf Shores. The seaside optimism that followed them back to St. Louis left them fitted with rose-colored glasses that blinded them to the danger they faced. Little did they know that Darnell-Wright had done his homework in their absence and was ready to spring a trap.

The clever brute rightly surmised that their best chance would be to strike when they least expected it. He'd cased their movements enough to know they were most comfortable and thus vulnerable when out in the sticks. Yeah, Sally and Michael really let their hair down in their favorite spot: St. Charles along the riverfront. There was a problem though. People like Darnell-Wright and his callous colleagues would stand out like a sore thumb on peaceful Main Street in St. Charles. The cunning thug decided they needed a distraction.

They didn't have to wait long for a diversionary tactic to happen along. That's because the anarchists figured they needed to extend the battleground beyond their strongholds in the inner cities. All across the country, the rioters spread out to the suburbs to hit the enemy where they lived. St. Louis was no different as the mobs fanned out to disrupt normally tranquil communities like St. Charles. It was only a question of timing.

Darnell-Wright and his evil pals were ready and waiting when Sally and Michael happened to be dining on Main Street when the agitators staged one of their so-called peaceful protests in the heart of old St. Charles. The organizers had played their cards close to the vest so there wasn't a heavy police presence when the unforeseen trouble started. Michael and Sally were enjoying an after-dinner drink when they heard the commotion outside. At first, it was just loud chanting about white privilege, social justice and the like. Michael stayed relatively cool and calm as he motioned to their waitress, "Could we have our check, please?"

It was dark outside but the street lights allowed them to see that the mob was quite large. They had bullhorns and various leaders took turns in agitating the marchers. One could feel the level of animosity climb as if the air had been charged with static electricity. The restaurant manager stood by the front exit, spread his arms apart and announced, "Folks, for your safety, we'd recommend that you stay put for now. I've contacted the police and help should be on the way shortly."

Michael signed their receipt and placed his credit card back in his wallet before leaning in to whisper in Sally's ear. "I doubt the police will offer much protection. Let's see if there's a back way out."

The restaurant manager spied their retreat and called out, "Sir, Ma'am, please stay in your seats, please."

Michael wasn't in the mood for useless debate, "Yes, in just a moment. I'm sorry but we really need to use the restroom." Once down the hallway and out of the manager's sight, they turned left and made their way to the exit. A steep wooden stairway led down to the parking lot that was on the same level as the river. They paid no attention to the concrete steps that continued downward behind them to the building's basement storeroom that rested below street level. They never saw it coming.

Sally screamed as she was jerked backward forcefully. A hand clamped down over her mouth and pulled her in close to a pair of whispering lips, "One word and I'll snap your scrawny, white neck."

Michael whirled around to see why Sally had screamed only to find himself eyeball to barrel with a .45 Smith & Wesson. A second thug cautioned, "Back off, cracker!" Michael stepped back and the two men cautiously backed down the short flight of steps with Sally in tow, all the time keeping the gun trained on Michael. Once at the bottom, he waved the gun in a circular motion to draw Michael forward. After a steady stream of vulgarity laced with numerous racial slurs, he ordered, "Don't get any ideas, Karate Man."

Michael calmly sized up the situation and concluded he couldn't fight back and take the chance of putting Sally in further jeopardy. He tried to buy some time. "So, we meet again."

"Dat's right. Only, this time you won't be pulling any of that karate crap on us or I'll pop a cap in your big, white ass."

Michael tried to sound nonchalant and confident, "Boy, you guys really hold a grudge." They just sneered at him. "It's not too late to forgive and forget."

He thrust the S&W toward Michael angrily, "Forget this!"

Michael maintained the voice of reason, "I can see why you're upset but, look fellas, we're not in St. Louis. The prosecutor here in St. Charles won't be so friendly. Kidnapping and brandishing a deadly weapon. Those are serious crimes. You could be looking at a very long stretch in state prison."

"Shut your pie hole!" He spat out more racial epithets.

The guy holding Sally smiled wickedly, "We won't be in St. Charles much longer."

This rattled Michael but he tried to hide his concern by changing the subject. "I'm surprised your other two pals aren't here."

The leering punk holding Sally let his hand drop down from her mouth to her breast and started fondling her. Rage crossed Michael's face and he lurched forward. The other thug violently swung his arm and brought the butt of his gun down on Michael, catching him just above his eyebrow. His knees buckled momentarily and blood from the deep gash flooded his eye. Sally's attacker laughed lustily before taking his ringing phone out of his pocket. "Yeah, we got their asses. We're out back at the bottom of the stairs. Right." He turned to Michael with a reptilian grin, "Don't worry, the gang's all here, bruh."

The other hood with the gun taunted Michael who he'd rendered momentarily defenseless. He pulled Sally's skirt up, "Ooh wee! Look at that fine thang! Prime white meat from Colonel Sanders." He belched a guttural, demonic laugh. "Check it out, bruh!"

Sally's malefactor released his grip over her mouth again; this time to invade her private parts. She threw all caution to the wind and screamed as loud as she could, "Police! Police! Help, police!"

"Go head. Scream all you want. All da pigs are up there. Can't hear you anyway." He pointed forward, "And none dose people down by the river would dare help y'all. Their white ass too scared."

Just then, a white panel van pulled up. Darnell-Wright hung his head out the front passenger window, "Put them in the back. Hurry up!" As soon as the doors closed, they sped off along Riverside Drive. He turned to peer into the back of the van, grinning like a kid in a candy store. "Mikey and Sally. Congratulations y'all. Heard about y'all getting hitched." Michael tried to reason with his captors once again. "Shut him up!" The two in the back gagged and tied him.

Sally pleaded, "Please, let us go. We won't tell anyone."

"Sally, Sally, Sally. It's been a long time, girl. Did you miss me?" He feigned forgetfulness, "Now, where were we?" She turned toward Michael and sobbed uncontrollably. "I'm sorry but Karate-Man ain't gone be no help this time." The smirk disappeared momentarily as he turned to his henchmen, "Is he clean?"

One of the men frisked him and pulled out his Glock, "Sorry man, we waz kinda busy, you know."

"Yeah, right. You waz busy checking out Sally." He turned to Sally with a smug look,

89

"Sorry, darling, but looks like your hubby got himself into a gun fight without a gun or even a knife. Can't even use some of those wicked karate chops being all tied up."

Michael struggled mightily to free himself but he was bound too tightly. Still, he caused such a ruckus that the two men in the back of the van had to flop on top to hold him down. Sally screamed, "Stop! Please stop!"

Darnell-Wright spoke mockingly, "Come on big fella. Save your energy. You're gonna need it." He turned back to Sally. "How was the honeymoon, girlfriend?" She whimpered and tried to look away. He grabbed his crotch and declared, "I've got a nice wedding present for you."

Michael could see through the rear windows that they'd jumped on I-70 East heading back toward the city of St. Louis. He kept track of their route as best he could, making mental notes when they took the Grand Avenue exit and passed the old water tower before winding through nearby streets in one of the deadliest parts of North St. Louis. Before leaving the van, they put linen sacks over Michael and Sally's heads to block their vision. Michael took odd relief in concluding that, perhaps, this meant they didn't intend to kill them.

He was correct but what they had in mind was, in some ways, worse. The four thugs ushered Michael and Sally up some stairs, through a creaky doorway and then down another staircase. When their hoods were removed, they found themselves in a dusty, dank basement lined with cobwebs and littered with fast food trash. The place smelled so rotten and sour it almost gagged them. It must have been abandoned because there was no electricity. The only light came from their flashlights and a battery-powered lantern.

Darnell-Wright had obviously thought things out ahead of time because he barked precise orders, "You two, untie him. And you, keep your gun on him and blow his brains out if he makes a move." With that accomplished, he pointed toward a post in the middle of the basement. The house must have been really old because the post and the support beam above were made of thick wood rather than steel. He waved his hand and the two thugs holding Michael backed him up against the post. Darnell-Wright tossed a couple of thick rolls of duct tape their way. "Strap him down good."

Michael looked like a mummy-in-progress when they finished. His arms were pinned to his sides and a good portion of his torso was covered by gray tape that was wrapped tightly around him and the wooden post. He was positioned to have a perfect view of the proceedings. Darnell-Wright ominously stroked his face where Sally had left the scars, "Hmmm, now where were we?" He motioned to his pals and two of them held Sally by her arms while the other ripped her dress off.

Michael screamed so loud it shook some dust from the rafters, "I'll kill you; you stinking bastard!"

"Shut him up." One of his henchmen wadded up a filthy cloth and shoved it into Michael's mouth. He secured it by wrapping a strip of duct tape around his head. Michael could only object with unintelligible, muffled grunts. "I don't care about the noise. Trust me, there's no one around to hear you anyway. But you shouldn't be messing up Sally's soundtrack, bruh," he grinned devilishly. "All right. Let's get this party started."

The guy with the gun tried to be funny, "What about us?"

"Don't worry. You'll get your turn. After I'm done."

One of the punks used a switch blade to cut off Sally's bra and then roughly tore off her panties. She remained oddly calm, perhaps not wanting to give them the satisfaction of sounding terrified. They pushed her to her knees in front of Darnell-Wright who stroked the scars on his cheek again, "Tape her hands behind her back." It didn't take much to restrain Sally since she was so petite.

When Darnell-Wright unzipped his pants and exposed himself, Michael must have been thinking, *At least Paul Kersey didn't have to watch them rape his daughter.* Nearly helpless, Michael made as much commotion as possible in his fettered condition. This distracted the four thugs momentarily. No one noticed when Sally curled her hands enough to slice a tiny notch in the tape with one of her fingernails. Darnell-Wright must have been thinking back to the way Sally had dug into his face and Michael had pounded him into the pavement because he turned mean. After insulting her womanhood and race, Darnell-Wright commanded, "Open your damn mouth!"

Molly defiantly replied, "Never!" and clenched her jaws together. One of the thugs standing behind her stepped up and clutched her head. He dug his thumbs into her cheeks and applied such pressure that Sally had to open her mouth. She surprised him by twisting her head in a lightning-fast motion and clamped down on his thumb with her teeth. He howled in pain and reared back to strike her hard.

Darnell-Wright shouted, "Stop! Not 'til I'm done with her!" The wounded perp backed off, cradling his bloody thumb with his other hand. Darnell-Wright turned to the third creep, "Gimme that gun!" Once in hand, he vowed to Sally, "Open up now or I'll blow your head off!"

Sally looked up at him with blood in her eyes, "I'd rather die." Michael raised another ruckus, such as he could. In that moment, Sally, who had been twisting her hands to expand the notch she'd cut in the tape, broke free and raked her claws across Darnell-Wright's privates as hard as she could.

The others could almost feel the excruciating pain through the girlish, high-pitched squeal that involuntarily escaped from his lungs like a wounded banshee. He grabbed himself and fell to the ground in a fetal position. Blood dripped from his hands as he rocked back and forth like a traumatized baby. The others rushed to his side but pulled up short. No one wanted to touch him while he was exposed, holding onto his bloody junk.

Sally instinctively rushed to escape but had trouble seeing once outside of the lantern's halo. The three thugs pounced before she could make her way up the stairwell and dragged her back down by her hair. Like a frenzied pack of wild dogs, they unleashed a brutal beating that almost drove frantic Michael to keel over. No longer driven by lust, they unleashed the full fury of their rage. She was already unconscious when Darnell-Wright recovered enough to intercede, "That's enough!" They paused momentarily and looked at him like hungry lions who wanted to continue feeding. "I said enough!"

"After what she did to you?"

"I ain't taking no rap for killing her. She ain't worth it." They stared in disbelief, perhaps because he was actually using his brain; something that never occurred to them.

"What about him? Let me at least pop a cap in Mr. Karate-Man."

"Ain't taking no rap for him either." The other three remained agitated, apparently unconvinced. Darnell-Wright showed that he was the brains of the outfit. "Listen fools! Right now, ain't no prosecutor in the city that will bust us for beating some white ass. That might not be so if we kill 'em."

"You gonna let 'em rat us out to the pigs?"

"Ain't nobody gonna believe them. If it comes to that, our lawyer will claim they're making up lies to harass us."

"I guess you're right."

"Hell yeah, I'm right!" Darnell-Wright again proved he was a thinking man's thug, "Get some bleach out of the van and clean up my blood. Don't leave a trace of evidence for these turkeys."

After wiping down Michael and Sally's still-unconscious body to remove any prints or DNA and bleaching away any trace of their presence in the basement, the four thugs turned to leave. Darnell-Wright stopped in his tracks and walked back to Sally's motionless body. He took care to cover his hands with rags and then rolled her onto her back. Then he spread her legs apart. He strutted right up to Michael and pointed back at the obscene pose. "See that there? If you go to the cops, that's what it will look like the next time we get together." Michael turned his head away in disgust. Darnell-Wright turned away to leave but stopped again, "One more thing." He swung his arm viciously and slammed the butt of his gun into Michael's temple.

When Michael regained consciousness hours later, there were a few shards of daylight peeking through holes in the boarded-up windows. It was enough for him to make out Sally's prone body. She was still unconscious. His heart raced as panic overtook him. Then he noticed her diaphragm was moving ever so slightly. Although his head was throbbing miserably, this sure sign of life energized Michael to struggle mightily against his restraints. It seemed to take forever and Michael had to stop and catch his breath numerous times but, finally, he made progress. The tape loosened enough that he was able to bend forward and grab the top row with his teeth. He attacked like a rabid dog until he produced a deep tear. After that, he swayed back and forth again and again elongating the tear until, finally, he was able to get one arm free.

He didn't know what to do. They had taken their phones and left Michael and Sally in a virtual war zone where people were more likely to kill than help them. Before he could contemplate how to seek help, Michael retrieved Sally's dress to cover her nudity and used some of the tape to secure the torn garment. Looking at her condition, he threw caution to the wind and picked her up in his arms. Still a little wobbly, he had to steady himself before climbing the stairs.

Once outside, he had to pause again to let his eyes adjust to the sunlight. Most of the other houses on the block were boarded up and abandoned too. Consequently, Michael started walking in the direction of the water tower that looked to be about a half-mile away. He started to panic when a car turned down the street and headed toward him. As it drew near, he could see that the driver was a big black guy with what appeared to be a nasty disposition. Reflexively, Michael turned away and headed toward one of the abandoned houses. Then a gruff voice called out, "You need some help, man?"

When Michael turned back around, the guy's eyes told the story. They seemed caring and sympathetic despite his hard features and scruffy stubble. "Yes, my wife needs to go to the hospital. She's hurt pretty bad."

"Hop in."

Michael stretched Sally out in the back seat and jumped up front in the passenger seat. "I don't know how to thank you."

"Don't worry about that. What hospital?"

"Barnes." He didn't need directions. Michael would have turned back to I-70 and taken Market to Grand to be safe but the man took the direct route over Grand saving precious time. The car was a rust bucket and, apparently, the AC was on the fritz. Michael didn't care. He was simply grateful. He tried to make conversation but had to speak loudly since the windows were down. "I'm Michael," he held out his hand.

"JB. Pleased to meet you."

"Man, I'm glad you happened along. Must be my lucky day."

"Luck doesn't have anything to do with it. I work the night shift. Come home the same time every morning."

"Night shift. You must be beat." JB looked at Michael with the big lump on his head and glanced back at Sally lying unconscious in the back seat. He served up some dry wit with a wan smile, "Looks like you're more beat than me."

Michael thought for a moment and broke out laughing. "Yeah, I guess you're right, JB." The awkwardness melted away. "How'd you happen to be driving by on that street?"

"I live there. Down at the end of the block." Michael blushed. "It ain't so bad." He laughed, "Don't have many neighbors to bother me." JB nodded slowly, "Not bad at all – if you don't mind a few drug dealers and crack heads."

Full of wonder, Michael mused, "I still say I was pretty lucky to run into someone as nice as you."

"I'm telling you, man. Ain't no luck about it. I'd call it the providence of God."

"Oh, you're a Christian?"

"Amen to that!"

Michael sighed with relief, "Me too. Thank you, brother." Michael looked heavenward, "And thank you too, Lord!"

"Hallelujah!"

"JB, you've really restored my faith in mankind. Here, I was worried that we might not get out of your neighborhood alive."

"Just be thankful that God brought us together. But don't ever be fooled. Getting killed in my neighborhood is an easy thing. Especially for a white dude."

They switched the topic of conversation for the rest of the ride. JB and Michael got to know each other better but mostly took the opportunity to build one another up in the faith. By the time they made it to the hospital, they seemed like old friends. JB gave Michael a big bear hug as attendants wheeled Sally into the emergency entrance on a stretcher. Hustling up the walkway, Michael stopped to wave goodbye, "Thank you so much, JB! Godspeed, brother!"

Those were the last good feelings Michael would experience for quite a while. The emergency care team treated Sally for numerous bumps, abrasions, contusions and three broken ribs. Thankfully, while her face was badly beaten and the whites of her eyes turned bright red from broken blood vessels, her skull wasn't fractured. Sally was admitted to the hospital's intensive care unit. There, she was placed on a ventilator to assist her breathing. Sally was stable but in a coma.

Part Two:

Make My Day

"You've got to ask yourself a question: 'Do I feel lucky?' Well, do ya, punk?"

(HARRY CALLAHAN IN DIRTY HARRY)

Chapter 7:

Michael's outlook on life plummeted like that of a man riding a roller coaster from hell. Sally had lifted him from the doldrums of loneliness and carried him to the top of the mountain. Then, everything came crashing down like the Twin Towers on 9/11. Enduring the trauma of witnessing her attack by a pack of vicious maniacs was bad enough but the aftermath was even worse. If only a glimmer of hope existed! Any slight progress could have buoyed his spirits but Sally languished without any sign of recovery. It drove him to the brink when the doctors asked about removing life support.

Every waking hour away from work was spent by Sally's bedside. Many nights, Michael even slept on a cot in her hospital room. This continued after she was transferred to a long-term care facility within the medical center near the hospital. They placed Sally in the section called rehabilitation which only incensed Michael all the more. *Rehabilitation, ha! Who ever heard of rehabilitating a vegetable?* He blanched at the thought and tried to make amends for his lack of faith by speaking to his bedridden wife, "I'm so sorry, Sally honey. I didn't mean it." Then he knelt down and turned to God in prayer. "Lord, I don't know if Sally can hear me but I know you're listening."

Michael knew that he'd have to change his routine or he'd lose his sanity. "Sally, I may not be here quite as often for a while but please don't think that I don't care. I do, more than ever! It's just that there's something I must do for you." He reached out and took her hand. Only the warmth gave any hint of life inside her. "I'm going to light a fire under the City Prosecutor somehow, some way. You deserve justice." If Sally were able to respond, she probably would have said no. She might have appealed to Michael to let it go so as to not put himself in harm's way.

Michael was not about to be intimidated despite the vulgar threat that Darnell-Wright had issued after their last encounter. Surely, he figured, *what else could he do to Sally now*? With no fear for his own safety, Michael went to the police and swore out a complaint against Darnell-Wright and the other three nameless individuals. It provided a much-needed boost that the cop who took his statement sounded quite sympathetic. "Hello, Mr. Wyatt, I'm Officer Morgan, Richard Morgan. I've been assigned to your case."

Michael hesitated and looked disoriented before finally extending his right hand. "Pleased to meet you, Officer."

Morgan replied rather gruffly, "What's the matter? Haven't you seen a black cop before?"

Michael turned red and sputtered, "Of course! No, no, it's not that. Not at all." He tried to compose himself, "It's just that I didn't know if you'd take offense to a handshake, you know, with the COVID thing and all."

"Relax Mr. Wyatt. I was just busting your chops," he snickered. Morgan reached out and offered a firm, solid grip. "Sorry but I've got a warped sense of humor."

"By the way, please call me Michael."

"Okay, Michael. You can call me Officer Morgan." He deadpanned for a second before chuckling and adding, "There goes my screwed-up sense of humor again. Richard's fine.

This put Michael at ease, "That's a rare commodity these days. Especially, among cops." Michael stopped long enough to ponder whether he might have offended Officer Morgan by generalizing. "I mean, you guys have had a pretty rough go of it for quite a while now."

"You're telling me," he laughed.

Michael told him the whole story from beginning to end and Officer Morgan filled out the police report dutifully. "This wasn't my first encounter with these animals." Michael glanced to catch any reaction to the use of such a pejorative term but there was none. He went on to chronicle their first attack on Sally. "This time they were determined to make good on their earlier threat."

"So, after the first run-in, you sought and were denied a restraining order?"

"Yes, they basically got off without even a slap on the wrist." Michael huffed, "To tell you the truth, the prosecutor's office treated us more like criminals than victims."

Morgan looked around to make sure there was no one within ear shot, "Doesn't surprise me one bit. I could tell you some stories," he rolled his eyes.

"What do you make of our prospects this time?"

Morgan lowered his head and shoulders with an apologetic look on his face, "I'm not going to lie to you." He whispered, "I don't think this outfit would indict Charles Manson if he were black." Michael's countenance fell sharply. "Don't give up hope. I'm gonna do my best."

"Thanks. I really appreciate your help."

"I'll call you by the end of the week with an update." Morgan looked at the report to make sure he'd filled out the form properly. Gazing at Michael's personal data he mused, "I would have never pegged you as a security guard."

"Why is that?"

"You look like a three-piece kind of guy."

"I don't know whether to take that as a compliment or an insult," he laughed.

"Just be thankful you're a private cop and not on the City's payroll."

On Friday, Michael was surprised when Officer Morgan showed up at his place of work. "Hey Michael, I hope you don't mind me dropping by during working hours. Phone calls are so impersonal."

"Hey no, it's great to see you Officer, I mean, Richard." Michael added anxiously, "Any luck with our case?"

"No, there's nothing official to report yet but I wanted to share something privately," he lowered his voice. "It's a slow process. Lots of red tape. However, I've been doing some legwork and turned up a few interesting things." Michael leaned in. "Got a line on the other three guys." Michael's eyes lit up. "They all go way back. Grew up in the same neighborhood and attended the same high school." Morgan gave Michael a sly look, "Notice I didn't say they graduated."

"Go figure."

"Anyway, I know who they are. Cedric 'Onion' Brown, Casey 'Beast' Billups and Cortez 'Lil C' Jenkins. The ring leader's full name is Darcy 'King KO' Darnell-Wright but lately he just goes by 'King.'"

Michael grabbed a note pad and pen, "Go over that once more."

"Whoa there, fella. I didn't come here so you could take notes. Just wanted to let you know I wasn't sitting on my thumbs."

"Sorry," Michael put the pad and pen away but made some mental notes. "I didn't mean to interrupt. Go ahead."

"There's not much more to say other than all four have long records. It's mostly petty, juvenile stuff but, more recently, they seem to be taking a shot at the big time."

"Where do they live? Do you have their addresses?"

"Yes, but I'm not going to share that information with you."

"What high school did they attend?"

"You've got a one-track mind, Michael." He looked deadly serious, "Let's get one thing straight. Don't go sticking your nose in where it doesn't belong. Leave it up to the police."

Michael knew better than to cut off his best source of intel, "Whatever you say, boss." He changed the subject without leaving it completely, "Where did they come up with those nicknames?"

"Two are self-explanatory. Cortez is the little guy and Casey the 'Beast' is the big one. Too bad he didn't stay in school and ball out. Would have made a great offensive lineman." Morgan shrugged and offered a crooked smile, "Not too sure about the other one. Maybe it's 'Onion's' funny-shaped head." He paused and looked sympathetically at Michael, "I think you know where Darnell-Wright got his name."

Michael quipped, "Yeah, unfortunately. As for Cedric Brown, maybe his feet smell like onions or he has bad breath."

After Officer Morgan left, one of Michael's fellow security guards approached him, "So, how do you know *Dirty Harry?*"

"What? Do you mean Officer Morgan?"

"Yeah, but his nickname is *Dirty Harry.*"

"How so?"

"He's old-school. Doesn't cut the crooks any slack. I hear he's been disciplined by the City several times." He grinned devilishly at Michael, "He's one of the good guys."

Morgan kept Michael abreast of developments in the investigation but the wheels of justice turned much too slowly to suit Michael. However, when he was just about at his wit's end, the glacially slow process lurched into high gear. Unfortunately, justice wasn't the outcome. Michael Wyatt was crushed when Sally's assailants were given yet another free pass. The prosecutor's office dropped the case for what they deemed was a lack of evidence. Michael was considered an unreliable, hostile witness and Sally couldn't speak up for herself. Cynical Michael figured that even her eyewitness testimony would have somehow been discounted.

This left Michael bound and determined to seek justice on his own. First, he tried searching online to track down the four thugs but nothing emerged. They seemed to occupy a shadow world beyond his reach. With nothing else to go on, Michael decided to set a trap to lure his prey. Twice before, they'd attacked people in deserted parking garages. If nothing else, he had an idea of the proximity where they liked to prowl. In what he thought was a flash of genius, inspired of course by *Paul Kersey*, he decided to pose as a homeless guy. On days off from work, he pursued this strange obsession around the clock.

It was too warm for a long overcoat but that didn't stop him from concealing his middle age and remarkable fitness with shabby, filthy, loose-fitting clothing. Like many street people, he donned a heavy woolen cap despite the late August heat. Maybe it served as a substitute for grooming in the absence of shampoo and showering. In any case, it contributed to a clever disguise along with his COVID mask and strategically-smudged dirt and grease around the rest of his face and on the backs of his hands. The hitch in his gate and hunched-over posture made him look twenty years older and pathetically vulnerable.

He parked his carcass here and there in the general vicinity of the two garages where they'd attacked before. Sitting slumped over on the sidewalk with his back to soot-stained, downtown buildings, he pretended to be drunk or sleeping. If that wasn't enough, he sweetened the pot by setting a tin can close by with some bills purposely sticking out. Much to his chagrin, some people dropped more money in his can during the daytime. A few unruly teens razzed him occasionally but most people simply ignored him.

Evening was a different story. The clientele changed dramatically after the business crowd went home. There were far less people on the street and the few remaining souls seemed quite sketchy. Some taunted him. Occasionally, others nudged or even kicked him as they went by shouting things like, "Get off the street old man!" or "Get yo drunk ass outta here!" Once he had to hold onto the can for dear life to keep his beggar's dough from being stolen.

This routine proved fruitless for the most part so, he limited his charade to a nighttime endeavor. The later it got, the better his prospects.

He noted how infrequently the police patrolled the area. It made sense though because there wasn't much to protect. Except for the immediate area around Busch Stadium on game days, it looked like St. Louis rolled up the sidewalks by 8:30. Oddly enough, the one time he was rousted by a cop, it turned out to be Richard Morgan. Michael didn't want to blow his cover or risk being banished by his conscientious cop pal so, he played the part and moseyed along without Officer Morgan ever knowing.

Michael thought he'd hit paydirt when he lurched aimlessly like a drunken sailor through the parking garage where the old man had been killed. Although he pretended not to notice, he was keenly aware that he was being stalked from behind. *Returning to the scene of the crime*, he thought. He reveled at the prospect of facing off with Darnell-Wright and his crew again. They really didn't practice a lot of stealth but why should they? He acted as if he was in a stupor, oblivious to his surroundings. When they got close, right behind him, one of the thugs yelled, "Here comes, old man!" and swung from the heels to take him out with one punch.

Michael raised his arm in an L-shape and blocked the attack perfectly while grunting out,

"Haaaaaaaa!" so loudly that it startled his three attackers.

One exclaimed, "What the?" but Michael cut him off before he could finish the sentence. He whirled so fast it looked like a blur when he delivered a devastating spinning backfist to the startled teen's temple. In just a glance, Michael saw that this was not "King KO" and company. Despite his instantaneous disappointment, his martial arts instincts ruled and, in one continuous motion, he reverse pivoted with his other arm and caved in the second thug's cheek bone with a well-placed elbow.

The third attacker produced a knife and lunged at Michael's mid-section. Thanks to his cat-like reflexes, Michael was cut but not badly wounded. Seeing that the game had risen to the next level, Michael responded with a weapon of his own. Borrowing a page from *Paul Kersey's* book on self-defense, Michael had crafted his own slapjack by filling the end of an old tube sock with AA batteries. Like King David facing Goliath, Michael swung the homemade slapper in a whirring circle above his head like a lasso. Although mesmerized by this archaic display, the thug prepared to ward off the attack. To his surprise, Michael didn't move in but released the twirling projectile at just the right point to fire it straight into his forehead. It hit the mark with a clunking sound and then fell to the ground making a clacking noise as several batteries were spread across the pavement.

Michael left the melee with all three perps lying unconscious. No longer encumbered, he strode away through the shadows like a power walker; only affecting his slumped-over limp when he crossed paths with an occasional stranger. As soon as he was in the clear, he called his friend, Richard Morgan. "Officer Callahan, I'd like to report a crime."

He noticed Michael's name on the caller ID, "Very funny. I appreciate the *Dirty Harry* reference but it's kinda late for these shenanigans isn't it?"

"This is no joke. You need to get over to that parking garage where the old man was killed by Darnell-Wright, right away."

"What are you talking about?"

"There are three perps lying on the ground on level one. You best get over there before they wake up."

"What did you do?"

"I didn't do anything. I just happened to see something as I walked by."

"Yeah, right."

"There's no time to argue. Get going."

"Okay but we're going to discuss this later."

Someone working high above the city for one of the local news stations spied the flashing lights atop Officer Morgan's cruiser as he sped down Market Street below. The savvy newsman's intuition told him to dispatch a camera crew to the scene which was less than a half-mile away. The whole thing was caught on camera and made for great television. It was all very mysterious but the reporter was able to gather that some kind of vigilante had surprised the thugs and made mincemeat out of them.

Michael couldn't help but be amused by seeing his pal's mug on TV as the reporter fired a barrage of questions at him. Officer Morgan deftly dodged most of them but couldn't fully conceal his discomfort. He was still worked up when he knocked on the door to Michael's condo. "Come in Richard. I've been expecting you."

"Wipe that smile off your face." Michael continued to grin as he ushered him to the kitchen table and offered him a Bud Light. "I'm still on duty." Michael sat down with his elbows on the table and cupped his chin in both hands, looking like a mischievous child who was proud of his work. "What the hell did you do?"

Michael could tell from his tone that his cop pal was in no mood for games so, he came clean. "I've been hanging out on the streets for the last week posing as a homeless guy."

Richard's jaw dropped. Flabbergasted, the only word he could manage was, "What?"

"I didn't break any laws and I was only minding my business."

"Do you think you're some kind of private eye? Working under-cover on a stakeout?"

"I'm just trying to find the guys who attacked Sally."

"You're damn lucky you only saw what happened and didn't get caught up in it."

"Maybe they were the lucky ones," he snickered.

"Okay, enough funny business. Do you know how dangerous that is?"

Michael shed his flippant attitude and matched the seriousness of the cop's demeanor. "If it's dangerous out on the streets, it's because you're setting the bad guys free." Michael paused to reconsider, "I didn't mean you personally. The City and that insane prosecutor have unleashed a veritable crime wave on our streets."

"You think I don't know that?"

"Richard, my wife's in a coma thanks to punks like the guys who tried to attack me tonight."

"So, it WAS you! You didn't just see it. You did it!"

"Yeah, it was me. Don't I have a right to defend myself?"

"You pretended to be a defenseless, old man! In our business, that's called entrapment."

"Well, I'm not in your business!" With eyes wide, he challenged Richard, "It's okay to attack a defenseless old drunk?"

"No, of course not."

"You should be thanking me."

"Thanking you? Michael, you took the law into your own hands!"

"If the cops can't protect us, who will? Damned right I took the law into my own hands."

"You hurt those guys really bad. Could have killed them."

"If I wanted to kill them, they'd be dead. I only used my hands on the first two. The last one drew a knife on me so, I clocked him with my slapper."

"Your hands could be considered deadly weapons. And, yeah, I saw that contraption you left behind. And the media did too. They're all over it. I suggest you forego the AA slapper." His eyes bored in on Michael. "What if they'd had a gun?"

"I guess I would have tried to disarm them."

"Don't even go there. Man, you shouldn't be out on the streets. It's too damn dangerous!"

"You ought to know, Richard."

"Yes, it's getting worse by the day. But you're on thin ice, man. The media's all over this. They're going to make you out to be a wild-eyed vigilante roaming the streets looking for innocent victims." He looked disgusted and helpless, "I can see the headlines now, 'Crazed Vigilante Literally Guilty of Assault and BATTERY.'"

"Knowing the media, you're probably right." Michael tried to make light of it. "Or they might say, 'Assault with BATTERIES.' So what? What's a little more fake news to go around?"

"It could land you in hot water, that's what." Morgan tried to reason with Michael, "Look, this will die down eventually. Just lay low and don't let it happen again."

"Oh, just let Darnell-Wright and his buddies off the hook again while Sally rots away?"

"We might not ever be able to put them away for what they did to Sally but I've been at this game for a while now. I can tell you this. With lowlife scum like Darnell-Wright and his crew, sooner or later, we'll get them for something."

"And as long as there's a corrupt, pro-crime prosecutor, they'll get off on that too."

"Nothing lasts forever. Just give it some time."

"Richard, I really appreciate what you're trying to do but I won't be able to rest as long as those four animals are free to prowl the streets."

Morgan hung his head low and shook it side-to-side. "There's only one way to stop me." Morgan raised his head. "You'll have to turn me in."

The conflicted cop knew he was fighting a losing battle. "I'm on your side, man."

"Then why are you fighting me?"

"I'm trying to protect you." Michael just stared at him blankly, completely unconvinced. "Look, I despise that prosecutor as much as you do. She doesn't have our backs for a minute. Sides with the perps every time. This crap about criminal justice reform is a lot of BS. It's an excuse to push a radical agenda through anarchy and violence. As for Black Lives Matter, she doesn't give a damn about black lives. Didn't shed a tear when we buried three fellow cops earlier this year. Two of them were black. Did their lives matter? Hell no, not to her!"

Morgan had worked himself into a frenzy and had to take a few deep breaths. "If I could get rid of her sorry ass today, I would." He paused again but couldn't seem to calm down. "I've been in her dog house for a long time. She's the one who labeled me as *Dirty Harry*. Thinks I'm an old dinosaur, a throwback to the bad old days. She'd like nothing better than to bust me down to a desk jockey or get rid of me altogether."

"Now, I see why you looked so uncomfortable in front of the TV cameras. I guess you need to lay low." Michael swallowed hard, "I'm really sorry that I put you in the spotlight tonight."

"Don't worry about it. I was already on her radar." Morgan smiled confidently, "She's on my radar too. I just know that commie wench is in cahoots with big money. Rumor has it that some of her political donors are nothing but rich, far-left loons."

"Listen Richard, I'll make sure not to drag you into the limelight again."

"I wish I could convince you to drop it altogether but, I know, I know, I'll save my breath. But please, please be careful." Michael started to explain how he'd take steps to be more cautious but Morgan cut him off, "I don't want to know."

"Okay, mum's the word."

"There is one thing, though. If you're going to be trolling the streets for monsters, please be prepared." Michael looked at him quizzically. "Take your damn gun with you next time."

"I don't want to shoot anyone."

"I know that but you better be prepared in case someone wants to shoot you. You may be tough, *Bruce Lee*, but you're not *Superman*."

Chapter 8:

Officer Morgan continued to fear for his friend's safety. He conveniently made a habit of patrolling the area around the two parking garages where Michael continued stalking under the guise of a homeless, old drunk. After several encounters, Michael did his old man shuffle over to the cop and whispered, "What are you doing, Richard? You're going to blow my cover."

"Sorry man but I can't stop worrying. This thing could really backfire on you." Michael looked both ways to make sure no one was watching them and tried to reassure Richard by pulling up his baggy shirt just enough to reveal the butt of a gun protruding above his waistband. "Oh Lord! Are you crazy?"

"What do you mean? You're the one who told me to arm myself."

"I know – but I hoped you wouldn't need to. Can't you just go home and leave this to me? I promise you that you'll be the first to know if I catch sight of your buddies."

"Do we have to go through this again?"

Richard exhaled forcefully to relieve the pressure, "No, I guess not." He shook his head regretfully, "I still don't like it."

The next day, Richard stopped by Sally's room at the medical center to talk to Michael. "How's she doing?"

One dismal syllable spoke volumes, "Same."

"Don't give up hope, man."

Michael's forced attempt to sound upbeat couldn't disguise his dejected spirit, "Yeah, I know. With God all things are possible."

"C'mon, Michael. What you just said is true!" Michael nodded half-heartedly. "Hey brother, let's share in a prayer." Richard put forth their petitions before God while adding, "In this and all things, thy will be done." He ended by asking God's blessings in Jesus' name.

"Thanks Richard. That's just what I needed. I appreciate it." A small but genuine smile crossed Michael's face. "I trust in the Lord. I know for certain that, no matter what happens, no matter where this situation leads us; God has our best interests at heart, always."

"Amen, brother! His top priority is always the salvation of our immortal souls." They sat together in peace and silence for quite a while before Richard spoke up. "There's something else I want to share with you."

"Oh, what's that?"

"It's about your undercover work," he said the last two words derogatorily."

"Oh boy, here we go again."

"No, I'm not here to talk you out of it but."

"Here's come the big but."

Richard brought Michael to attention, "You're wasting your time with this random homeless guy routine."

"How so?"

"You're never going to find these guys that way."

"And you know this how?"

Richard scooted close and lowered his voice, "I've got a line on these guys." Michael held his breath. "Remember when I told you Darnell-Wright and company weren't satisfied with small potatoes anymore?" Michael nodded anxiously.

"Well, it appears they've decided BLM is their ticket to bigger and better things. A couple of 'em have already been arrested for protesting twice and released."

"Huh?"

"They're not really interested in social justice reform or anything like that but I guess they think they can fast-track their ambitions by hitching their wagons to the protesters."

"Sorry but I don't follow the logic."

"I'm sure you remember how they used the St. Charles protest as a diversion that allowed them to kidnap you and Sally." Anger flashed in Michael's eyes as he nodded sharply. "Similarly, the ongoing riots can provide cover for them to expand into all kinds of related criminal enterprises like looting and extortion. As they've already found out, they risk very little chance of being put away permanently as, you know, peaceful protesters," he mocked.

"Ah, now I see." It didn't take long for Michael's puzzled look to return. "What does this have to do with me and my undercover work as you called it?"

"Mind you, I'm not encouraging anything but just wanted you to know that your boys have moved onto greener pastures. You're wasting your time hanging out around downtown parking garages."

"So, you think I should hit the protest scene?"

"Absolutely not! Unless you really want to flirt with danger."

Michael soberly replied, "I hear you," and thoughtfully scratched his chin, "Thank you." No sooner was Richard relieved when Michael dropped this bomb, "I'll be glad to toss this filthy get-up in the can. I guess I'll have to look for something in black with matching goggles."

"Not funny."

Michael seemed to look right through his nervous cop pal, "Not joking." Then, with a voice of complete nonchalance, "Don't worry, I'm not thinking of going undercover just yet."

"Good."

"I'll just hang around the fringe and see if I can spot Darnell-Wright and his posse."

"Please don't. If you haven't noticed, these aren't peaceful protesters." Michael nodded and laughed angrily under his breath. It sounded weirdly sinister to Richard. "Even if you don't come across Darnell-Wright and his demented buddies, you'll be in grave danger. There's no controlling these mobs."

This went in one ear and out the other. "Let's see, where do I start?" Michael snapped his fingers, "How about North County? Ferguson seems like the logical choice. If that doesn't work, Florissant is close by and, from what I gather on social media, appears to be one of the new hot spots."

"Got it all figured out, eh smart guy?" With a thick air of caution, Richard offered this warning. "North County is out of my jurisdiction so; I won't be around to help."

Michael smiled wickedly, "I know."

Michael rarely needed to take his car out of the garage except when he drove down Market to Grand to visit Sally. His condo, workplace and parking garage hunting grounds were all within walking distance. His new routine required piling up a lot more mileage. His visits to Sally became a little more frequent. Her condition hadn't changed but there was an ulterior motive. Michael scoped out the situation carefully before taking the leap, figuratively and literally.

Sally's room was on the fourth floor of a ten-story facility. Her window faced away from Grand Avenue and the main parking lots. By chance, it was perfectly situated to provide peace and privacy. Her room was at the end of one hallway where it intersected with another perpendicular walkway leading back toward the main elevators. Her window was at the end of one face of the building where it formed a corner with the adjoining section that jutted out about twenty feet further. Even in the daytime, it was hard to see the drain pipe that ran down the length of the corner because of the shadows.

Like any medical facility, there were security cameras all over the place; in the hallways, at nurse's stations, the lobby, exits and across the parking lots. However, there were no cameras in the rooms due to cost and privacy concerns and there was no reason for surveillance on the backside of Sally's wing where there wasn't an exit and virtually no foot traffic nearby.

One night, the sun was going down around 7:45 when Michael signed in at the lobby. He made sure to be noticed at the nurse's station on the fourth floor. By this time, he knew the routine well. The nurse on duty came by promptly at 8:00 to check on Sally's vitals, make sure she had plenty of liquid nutrition, dispose of any waste and adjust her position to prevent bed sores. Unless the monitor sounded an alarm, there wouldn't be another round until midnight.

Tactically, Michael had visited frequently enough to become familiar to regular staff members. He also made sure it was commonplace for him to stay for long periods of time. Sometimes, he would pretend to have fallen asleep in front of the TV only to be rousted by the midnight nurse. Occasionally, he would say he wanted to spend the night on the couch rather than making the drive home.

On this night, shortly after the 8:00 rounds were over, Michael turned up the volume on the TV enough so that any passersby in the hallway would hear and assume he was engrossed in a football game or movie. He donned a pair of leather work-gloves before sliding the window open. When he stretched out and grabbed the heavy metal drainpipe, he was pleased at how sturdy it felt and noted how well it was tied down with thick brackets every ten feet or so. Still, it took some courage to trust that it could hold his weight. If it broke away, he wouldn't have a chance.

As a precaution, he took out the thin but strong black polyester rope he'd hidden in the bottom of a bag of keepsakes he'd brought in to supposedly brighten up Sally's room. He anchored it around the base of the toilet, opened the window and let the rope drop down to the ground below. He'd measured precisely to have just enough length to reach almost to the grass. If the drainpipe didn't hold, he could latch onto the rope. More importantly, this would give him an easier way of climbing back up.

He took a deep breath and backed out through the window. Thankfully, the rough brick exterior provided good traction for his feet. The most harrowing part was transferring one hand from the window sill to the drain pipe and then the other. He kept a close eye on his safety line, the rope that he'd dropped purposefully close to the corner drainpipe to conceal it. When the drain pipe held steady and secure, he breathed a sigh of relief before shimmying down.

It didn't take much effort descending but coming back up would be another matter. He hoped the rope along with the advantage of the brick walls at right angles to one another would allow him to scale four stories like a mountain climber. Not wanting to leave much to chance, Michael had practiced wall climbing at a local *Sky Zone* several times.

It took him less than a half hour to hop on I-70 West and get to Ferguson where he spent over an hour scoping out the situation. Dressed in black from head to toe with his mask and a wool cap pulled down low, Michael was able to avoid drawing attention to himself by staying in his car. There were no full-blown riots but lots of suspicious characters were milling about along West Florissant. Tension floated in the air, as if there was a powder keg just waiting for a spark to ignite it. After making numerous passes and pulling into a few parking lots of fast-food joints and liquor stores and with no sign of Darnell-Wright or the others, Michael headed back.

There was very little going on at ten o'clock in this neighborhood. Most visitors had left and it seemed like a ghost town except for the hustle and bustle at the emergency entrance to the hospital next door. Still, Michael was on edge never having tried this before. Scaling the wall was one thing but *what if Sally's monitor had gone off? What if some conscientious nurse had wandered by to say hello to him? What if some random groundskeeper or security guy had happened upon the rope dangling from Sally's window?*

Thinking of Sally and her condition made Michael set his jaw. *In for a penny, in for a pound.* It was now or never so, he put on his gloves, grabbed the rope and shaped his body into an L with each foot planted firmly against one of the intersecting brick walls. He quickly realized he never would have made it back up using the drainpipe alone but the rope really helped. It gave him the leverage to step and pull methodically, gaining altitude at a pretty good clip. About halfway up, when the height became dangerous, something close to panic set in.

He paused and drew a deep breath. The climb had become physically taxing. It wasn't so much his back and legs but his biceps were burning as if he'd attempted too many curls. There was no turning back. Michael had to either keep going or slide back down and relinquish any hope of catching Sally's attackers. Partly to avoid the embarrassment of explaining his hair-brained scheme but mostly for Sally's sake, he continued on.

A second wind lifted Michael as if he'd tapped into a hidden reserve of adrenalin. When he grabbed the window sill and peered into Sally's room, he was relieved to see that nothing had changed. He climbed in, gathered up the rope and shut the window. After some careful thought, Michael hid the rope in the linen closet under some heavy blankets that wouldn't be needed for a couple of months. He'd accomplished his mission in under three hours. Although he didn't find his targets, he was pleased at the success of his trial run.

Michael visited his hunting grounds in Ferguson several times to no avail. He did so without repeating his mountaineer routine, figuring he'd only go to that extreme if there was a good chance of striking paydirt where he might need an alibi. As August turned to September, he gave up hope that Ferguson might be fertile ground. He became despondent to the point where he didn't even bother expanding his efforts to Florissant. That is, until he heard the news about things turning violent along Lindbergh Boulevard.

Florissant had endured a nightly routine of so-called peaceful protests along Lindbergh near the police station for week-after-week. It certainly wasn't peaceful but the violence occurred so routinely that it had almost become blasé. This changed when the latest purported injustice occurred where a cop in a faraway city had the audacity to use deadly force against a knife-wielding attacker. BLM and Antifa promised to ramp up the mayhem and brazenly announced that Florissant would be their first target.

Michael sensed a golden opportunity and prepared accordingly. Dressed in black, he visited Sally as night fell. This time, having experienced a flawless trial run, Michael repeated his great escape, only this time more efficiently and with greater confidence. Using more stealth this time, he parked in St. Ferdinand Park about a mile away from the melee and walked down subdivision side streets toward the ruckus. He warily approached the riot that reminded him of the type of unfettered lawlessness and violence he'd seen streaming through his TV from places like Portland, Chicago, Seattle, Atlanta, Louisville and New York.

He exercised great caution to maintain some distance while edging ever closer to get a better look. Using cars and bushes for cover, he surveyed the crowd through a compact pair of binoculars. It was tough to see well because everyone was in motion, tossing bottles, hurling rocks and taunting the police officers. He was about to give up when he turned to look north up Lindbergh on his side of the street across from the police station. A few of the rioters had spilled across Lindbergh to loot some of the businesses. Most were restaurants and small retail shops.

He keyed in on a nearby strip mall that featured a jewelry store and a pawn shop.

Something caught his eye ever so briefly as his field of vision passed the jeweler's storefront. *No, it can't be!* Michael feverishly swung the binoculars back to the small group of looters breaking through the windows. Desperation set in as he frantically tried to recapture the image that he thought he'd seen but to no avail. Then he froze, blinked his eyes and zeroed in. *Yes!* Front and center, about to enter the jeweler's shattered storefront was one of Sally's attackers; the small one, "Lil C" Jenkins.

His first reaction was to dial 911 but any hope faded when he glanced across the street. Every cop in the city of Florissant was already occupied and knee-deep in trouble. Calling his pal Richard wouldn't help either. By the time he could get there, the looters would be long gone. With no other options at hand, Michael decided to move in closer. Perhaps in his dark outfit he'd blend in or at least not draw Jenkins' attention in the midst of the chaos.

Most of the action was on the other side of Lindbergh so, it helped to temper the risk. All Michael wanted to do was get close enough to get some video that could be used to put Jenkins and the other looters away. Michael took out his phone and hit the video button. He had to lift his goggles up to his forehead to see well enough to capture them in the act. In all the confusion, he didn't even notice that his mask had slipped below his chin.

By this time Jenkins and his crew were inside ransacking the jewelry cases. The other looters that had crossed Lindbergh were busy inside the pawn shop pilfering everything in sight, including guns. Since no one was left outside on this side of the street, Michael made the bold move of stepping right up to the shattered window to get a good view of the crooks. Unfortunately, the light from Michael's phone caught Jenkins' eye. He turned and immediately recognized his nemesis. He nudged the other two thieves and shouted some vulgar racial slurs, "Get him!"

Michael slammed his phone in his pocket and sprinted for the nearby subdivision. He hurdled several fences and weaved his way through unsuspecting folks' back yards in an effort to elude the three thugs who were in hot pursuit. Michael didn't even consider knocking on anyone's door since he knew no one in their right mind would respond with the riots occurring just blocks away. His best chance was to make it back to his car but, as fate would have it, his toe caught the top of a chain link fence.

It was the last yard that bordered the grounds of dark and deserted St. Ferdinand Park. He gathered himself as quickly as possible and resumed his frenetic flight toward his parked car but in those few seconds while he was on the ground, his frenzied pursuers were able to close the gap. The only option left was to turn and fight. He quickly sized up his three opponents. One had a baseball bat, the other a pipe and "Lil C" appeared to be unarmed. They circled him like a pack of hungry wolves waiting for the right opportunity to pounce.

The guy with the pipe made the first move and took a vicious swing at Michael's head. He deftly ducked the blow and shot back with an upper cut that buried deep into his attacker's mid-section. Then he crushed his nose back up toward his brain. The young man with the bat seized the chance to come from behind and slammed the Louisville Slugger onto Michael's back making a loud, sickening smacking sound. Fortunately for Michael, the blow landed flush across his back where the brunt of the force was absorbed by muscle rather than his ribs or spine.

Michael couldn't help but sense the height of irony. The bat-man was a woke white guy supposedly crusading for black lives while looting a black-owned business. Brimming with

140

overconfidence as he looked down at Michael, he unleashed a series of racial slurs as he denounced Michael's white privilege. One white guy was taunting another white guy as he prepared to bludgeon him to death.

The attacker reared back to finish Michael off with a head shot but was surprised by the swiftness of his recovery and reaction. Still down low to the ground, Michael spun as if he were breakdancing and knocked the young man to the ground with a devastating leg sweep. In one continuous motion, Michael pounced and delivered a crunching blow to the thug's solar plexus rendering him helpless, gasping for breath.

This time, Michael didn't give "Lil C" the chance to attack from behind. He snatched the baseball bat and whirled before Jenkins could jump him. Michael's better nature had no chance against his dark side. Thinking of Sally, an evil stare seemed to possess his countenance, "So, we meet again."

Jenkins was nothing but a punk but didn't seem phased by the look on his malevolent foe's face. He was so bold as to offer this incendiary taunt, "Yeah – shame yo sweet little blonde thang ain't with you."

This so enraged Michael that he raised the bat high over his head and prepared to pound the little freak into the ground, "Rot in hell!"

Quick as a cat, Jenkins drew a handgun and thrust it toward Michael, "You first." Michael froze as he stared down the little thug with the smug, reptilian smile. "Well, well – what you say now, Karate-Man?"

Jenkins made a fatal error. He paused to relish the moment before pulling the trigger. He underestimated Michael's resolve and lightning reflexes for the last time. Michael answered stoically, "Goodbye," as he produced a gun of his own and shot "Lil C" point blank, right between the eyes.

It all seemed so surreal. One attacker was still unconscious and the other had his eyes squeezed shut as he struggled to recover from having the wind knocked out of him. Shock overcame Michael as his adrenaline rush ebbed. Still, there was no remorse; only the stark realization that he was a killer. His thoughts must have run the gamut. *Murder or self-defense? Hadn't he stalked his prey? But he tried to run away. Surely, Jenkins would have killed him.* He could only have been left with one thought as Sally came to mind: *mission accomplished.*

It's funny how our brains work sometimes. Michael suddenly recalled a TV show from his youth. It was an old, black-and-white western starring Richard Boone as a gunman for hire named Paladin. The show's title came from his business card. It featured a silhouette of a chess piece, the knight or horse, with the caption, *"Have Gun – Will Travel."* Normally, hired gunmen were the bad guys but, in Paladin's case, he was the hero who always came to the aid of the downtrodden and disadvantaged.

Yeah, maybe Michael was the hero after all. The jeweler and pawn shop owner would surely think so. Would Sally? Maybe not but Jenkins would never rape or kill again. *Good riddance!* Michael's actions revealed where he came down on the subject. He must have figured he needed a calling card like Paladin. Reaching into his tube sock slapper, he grabbed one of the AA batteries, taking care not to leave fingerprints or DNA and set it on Jenkins' chest.

There was no more time for self-examination. Michael pulled up his mask and placed his goggles over his eyes to conceal his identity before the two injured thugs could get a better look at him. He could only hope that they'd been too preoccupied with getting their butts kicked to focus on his face. In any case, he knew that the only guy who could definitely identify him was dead. Just to be safe, he left his headlights off until his license plates were out of range of the two guys still on the ground.

Richard's prediction came true. The media put two and two together and created a serial vigilante based upon the clue Michael had left on Jenkins' dead body. The headlines trumpeted, "Crazed AA Vigilante Turns Killer." The rest was pure fantasy but it fit the ongoing narrative well. The suspect, surely a white supremacist, stalked the innocent protesters while badly injuring two and killing one in cold blood. There was no mention of self-defense. No one questioned why the supposed victims were found a mile away from the site of the, in their words, peaceful demonstration.

The local news reporter who interviewed the two survivors in the hospital gave them free rein to label Michael as a bloodthirsty, white maniac bent on waging a race war. The reporter didn't note the irony of one of the supposed victims being white. Thankfully, for Michael's sake, they couldn't describe him other than to say he was a white dude dressed all in black with wicked karate skills. They lamented the loss of their dear friend and extolled his virtue as a model citizen fighting for equality and social justice. The media ran with their narrative and basically bestowed sainthood upon Cortez Jenkins.

Michael fumed as he thought about how the media's newly anointed saint had helped to savagely beat Sally. He wanted to call in sick the next day but knew better than to break from his normal routine in a way that might draw attention. He intended to lay low and his plan appeared to work since no one from law enforcement contacted him. That is, except for his friend, Officer Richard Morgan. "Come on in, Richard. I've been expecting you."

"You've taken this to a whole new level." Richard had that look of resignation that a high school football team gets when they're down by six touchdowns at the start of the second half. "Do you expect me to keep quiet?" Michael stared back with a do-what-you-have-to-do look on his face. Richard erupted, "Did you have to leave that battery as your calling card?" He swung his right fist and punched the palm of his left hand. "The media's all fired up and now the cops are involved. There'll be a damn task force set up to hunt you down!"

Michael slumped down on the couch with elbows on knees and chin resting in his hands. "Do you want to hear what happened?"

"It's too late for that. A man is dead."

"A lowlife scum, a vicious animal is dead." Richard exhaled loudly and collapsed into an easy chair, ready to hear his friend out. Michael took a while to collect himself and then swept back his hair. "I didn't go there to kill the guy. When I spotted him and his pals, they were busting into a jewelry store. I tried to take some video so that you could put them away. Jenkins recognized me and the three of them chased me down and tried to kill me." Michael hung his head. When he looked up at Richard, his eyes were red and moist. "They attacked me with a pipe and bat. Then Jenkins pulled his gun on me. I had no choice! If I hadn't shot him, he would have killed me for sure."

Richard talked through steepled fingers, "Okay, I get it. Settle down and tell me the rest of the story; everything that happened." When Michael finished, Richard seemed satisfied but couldn't swallow one bitter pill, "Why the battery? What in the hell were you thinking?"

"I don't know. It seemed like a good idea at the time." He paused and sounded apologetic, "Something came over me. It felt like I was on a crusade – fighting for the little guy; all the helpless, innocent victims who didn't ask for the violence – like Sally." He paused again to reflect and admitted, "I guess I also wanted to send a message to Darnell-Wright, Brown and Billups. You know, to let them know I'd be coming for them too."

Richard shook his head, "Sheesh! Have you ever heard of the element of surprise?"

"I guess I really blew that, eh?"

"You may be coming for them but I can assure you that the media is coming for you. That means the police will be on the hunt too."

"Don't worry. I have the perfect alibi. I was visiting Sally the whole time." He went on to explain how he'd left the medical center out the window and returned the same way without detection.

"That's great but you've left some damning clues too."

"How so?"

Morgan demonstrated his cop's mind, "They know they're looking for a martial arts guy." Michael gulped. "Let's hope they don't trace the events back to you and your first encounter with Jenkins and his pals in that parking garage."

"You're right. I'll have to be prepared if they ever catch up with me and pursue that line of questioning."

"Here's another thing. You better clean your phone."

"Oh yeah! The video I shot of them looting the jewelry store could do me in." Although momentarily distracted, Michael's haunting thoughts returned. "I didn't want to kill the guy." He paused again and ruefully admitted, "Thinking of Sally, I guess a part of me did."

"Don't go there, my friend. It was self-defense."

"Easy for you to say. You don't have blood on your hands." Michael immediately regretted saying this.

"Hey pal, I have as much at stake here as you. I'm complicit as long as I keep my mouth shut. I could easily be considered an accessory."

"I'm so sorry, Richard. It's not too late for you to do the right thing and turn me in."

"Right thing? You did the right thing. Otherwise, I'd be mourning your death. Jenkins was a murderous, remorseless hoodlum. It was self-defense. It's way too late for me to turn back. I'm with you all the way."

Chapter 9:

In the days that followed, any remorse that Michael might have felt was overwhelmed by righteous anger. The media had a heyday with the story and squeezed every drop of sensationalism out of it that they could manage. Michael didn't mind being made the villain but he was incensed by their portrayal of Cortez Jenkins as an amalgamation of Gandhi, Nelson Mandela and Mother Theresa rolled into one. Knowing that Jenkins' death was justifiable, Richard kept a tight lid on Michael's secret. With no other leads, Michael was home free and facing no heat from the authorities. Richard counseled him sternly, "You've dodged another bullet. Don't mess it up. Lay low and this too shall pass."

Michael knew better than to argue with Richard. However, what Officer Morgan took as compliance was only patience. Secretly, Michael was thankful to have come up with the perfect alibi. That's because he knew it would come in handy in the future. He had no intention of letting up until Sally received her justice, paid in full by the other three.

Michael smiled at the thought that Darnell-Wright must have guessed that he'd meted out retribution to Jenkins. However, even if DD-W was onto Michael, he couldn't blab to the police without bringing suspicion upon himself. He'd gotten off on the so-called lack of evidence with Michael Wyatt declared a hostile witness and knew better than to stir that pot again. Maybe he'd lost the element of surprise but Michael felt he'd gained a psychological edge.

Officer Richard Morgan's head nearly exploded the next time he and Michael sat down to catch up over a few Budweisers. That's because Michael revealed his true intentions, "I need your help."

"Shoot."

"I don't think it's a good idea for me to hang out around the riots."

"Agreed."

"So, I need you to help me track down the other three."

Richard hit the roof, "Like hell!"

"C'mon, Richard. You know this won't be over until they're all in jail or dead."

"You're out of your mind! You're the one who's going to wind up in jail or dead."

"That's the chance I'm willing to take."

Richard was about to flip out but the longer he stared at Michael, the clearer it became that nothing could change his mind. "I'd like nothing more than to see those guys behind bars but NO MORE KILLING! Do you hear me?"

"I hear you," Michael wasn't rattled in the least, "and I won't kill anyone unless I have to. I promise."

Richard spewed thick sarcasm, "Oh, that makes me feel much better."

"You can help me so that I don't have to kill them."

"And just how am I supposed to do that?"

"You can help me track them down, one-by-one." Michael smiled enthusiastically like a wide-eyed kid, "All we have to do is catch them in the act of committing a crime."

"Oh, is that all? And if they don't cooperate?"

"Kidnap them and force them to confess."

"Wow, you really are insane, Michael!" He looked at him like he was talking to a mental patient. "That would not only be damn near impossible but highly illegal. Would never stand up in court."

"It's worth a try. If that doesn't work, there are other ways."

"Really?"

"Yeah, for example, we could turn them against one another. They might rat each other out to protect their own butts. Might even do the job for us and knock each other off." Richard's jaw dropped but Michael innocently shrugged and added, "Worth a try."

"If you ask me, Michael, you're a few slices short of a whole pizza."

"Hey, I'm just trying to follow your orders. No more killing? Okay. These guys are criminals, right? You're a cop who's supposed to fight crime. I'm just a concerned citizen trying to help you out."

"It's getting deep in here, man." Richard wagged a finger at Michael. "I do like one thing though. At least you're trying to do this the legal way." The officer brought his palms together with his fingers pointing toward Michael. "I'll tell you what. I'll give this some thought but, in the meantime, lay low."

This is where I entered the fray even though I hadn't met Michael Wyatt or Richard Morgan yet. Like everyone else, I was hopelessly hooked on what had become the hottest local news story about the anonymous vigilante wreaking havoc on our darling peaceful protesters. As a local radio talk show host, I had a stake in the game. However, as usual, I marched to the beat of a different drummer.

My friends knew me as Dylan Rooney but listeners referred to me by my moniker, "Rambo" Rooney. It was a fitting title since I'd earned a reputation as a loose cannon who'd stop at nothing to demolish the fake news media. My favorite targets were insane liberals, loathsome political hacks and the mainstream media whom I'd vociferously labeled as our greatest enemy long before Donald J. Trump ever took office.

I considered myself an old-school journalist who formed opinions based upon facts. I'd dug into everything I could find on the vigilante and his so-called victims and reached a conclusion diametrically opposed to the sheeple that occupied every other corner of the local news establishment. To me, the vigilante looked like a hero and his victims appeared to be thugs with long criminal histories. Consequently, I started referring to the vigilante as an avenging angel.

154

This drove my competitors nuts but they'd learned to ignore me. Too many had found out the hard way that I'd chew them up and spit them out if they tried to engage me in a debate while armed with nothing more than unsubstantiated narratives and vapid talking points. Nevertheless, they listened to my show religiously to harvest ideas and didn't mind stealing if they came across something they liked. Such was the case with our anonymous boogey man.

They pilfered the name Avenging Angel and splashed it across the news as if it was their own novel invention. That's where the similarity stopped though. In their context, Avenging Angel was a highly derogatory term. They painted AA as a misguided religious fanatic driven by racially-motivated, right-wing extremism. In an effort to generate maximum fearmongering, they painted AA as a Nazi and card-carrying member of the KKK. Of course, they knew he had to be a Trump supporter.

I caused heads to explode when I countered by referring to the Bible to cast angels in a positive light. I told the story from 2 Kings 6 where the King of Syria suspected a traitor in his midst who was providing intelligence to the King of Israel. When he learned that it was the Prophet Elisha who was warning Israel's ruler, the King of Syria amassed his troops and sent them to Dothan to trap Elisha. The Prophet's servant was gripped with terrible fear when he awoke to see that they were surrounded by a host of enemy troops and lamented, "What shall we do?"

Elisha calmly replied, "There are more with us than them." Then he prayed for God to open his servant's eyes and the servant was allowed to see that the mountains were filled with God's protecting angels who were arrayed as great warriors atop chariots of fire.

To make matters worse for my detractors, I compared the victims and other rioters to demons possessed by another sort of celestial being: evil angels in service to Satan. Rather than fearmongering, I tried to boost the confidence of the faithful by highlighting the power of Almighty God and His holy angels. For this, I referred to 2 Kings 19 where Assyrian King Sennacherib had it in for Israel's King Hezekiah. The latter knew his armies were no match for the bloodthirsty, cruel Assyrians who had already conquered many lands and peoples. Thus, King Hezekiah turned to God in prayer. The Lord answered resoundingly by sending a solitary angel who single-handedly killed 185,000 Assyrian warriors.

This approach not only assuaged my listeners but provided me with personal comfort and confidence too. With everyone else in town aligned against me, I could have felt outnumbered and alone. However, I had two things on my side that were insurmountable: God and the truth. While others bashed the Avenging Angel as a menace to society, I hailed him as a crusading crime fighter.

My voice was mostly drowned out by the liberal crowd but I persisted anyway. In addition, I openly accused my crafty competitors with plagiarism but they still took credit for the catchy moniker I'd invented. It didn't matter much though because we'd unleashed a veritable force of nature. The saga of the Avenging Angel took on a life of its own. Love him or hate him, the public was hungry for every morsel of information they could get on the vigilante. AA proved to be very accommodating in serving up new exploits to satisfy their ravenous appetites.

Richard Morgan didn't want to give Michael a chance to fall back into his bad, dangerous habits. Thus, he took it upon himself to implement Michael's plan as a solo act. Since he knew the address and whereabouts of Michael's three remaining targets, he decided to tail them to try to catch them in the act as Michael had suggested. First on the list was "Onion" Brown. It didn't take long for Morgan to get a line on the habitual reprobate. When he wasn't thieving or shaking someone down, Brown had a penchant for drugs and the ladies. That, along with his hair-triggered temper made for a volatile mixture.

One night, while they were both flying high on booze and dope, one of his frequent female companions fretted over how she'd erroneously assumed "Onion" was committed to her beyond something purely physical. She'd gotten wind of some of Cedric Brown's other dalliances and took him to task. Neither had a clue that Richard Morgan was staked outside the young lady's rundown brick flat on the city's old northside. The stealthy officer patiently waited for Brown to step out of line and he didn't disappoint.

"Onion" erupted with a tirade laced with disgustingly misogynistic insults meant to put his pushy playmate in her place. Firing back with a few choice words of her own, the screeching siren made the mistake of punctuating her retort with a hard slap to Brown's face. The fiery exchange was loud enough that the noise coming through the open window put Morgan on red alert. He burst out of his cruiser and rushed up the stairs as Cedric Brown flew off the handle drawing screams of pain and anguish from his lady friend.

Morgan didn't bother to knock since it was obvious the young woman was in great distress. The door was locked so, the officer instinctively laid his shoulder into it so heavily that it tore away from the frame. He flew into the next room and yelled, "Stop! Police!" The woman had been knocked to the floor with such force that her mouth was bloody and her face had already begun to swell. She looked a fright with her hair tousled wildly, tank top nearly torn off and tears mixed with mascara flowing down her face in obscene black rivulets. Brown shot his hand over to the night stand and thrust open the top drawer. Now, totally in character as the black *Dirty Harry* and serious as a heart attack, Morgan dared Brown, "Go ahead, make my day."

"Onion" thought better of it and slowly recoiled from the night stand. It was a tense situation as Morgan spied the gun Brown had tried to retrieve. He moved to put himself between Brown and the gun while shielding the battered girl he'd rescued. He barked at Brown, "Back up against that wall and don't make a move!"

Suddenly, another voice caused Morgan to drop into a crouch with his firearm extended toward the bedroom door. He came so close to unloading his clip that it made his knees tremble when he recognized Michael Wyatt. The unexpected interloper didn't even glance at Richard. Instead, Wyatt's eyes were riveted on Cedric Brown. "You like abusing women, don't you?"

Looking at his profile, Richard couldn't comprehend the look on Michael's face but he should have had a clue from Brown's expression which was one of sheer terror. Wyatt sprang like a jungle cat before Richard could intercede. Using his left leg for a base, Michael extended his right leg and unleased three devastating blows in split-second succession. First, he thrust his heel into Brown's chest nearly collapsing a lung. His right thigh, at a ninety-degree angle to his left leg, didn't move but he cocked his foot by whipping his lower right leg back at the knee. Whap, he slung the upper arch of his foot into Brown's jaw, reloaded and slammed his heel into the stunned man's nose.

Brown collapsed in a heap in front of Michael who leered at him with a sick, satisfied smile. Captivated by the sheer quickness of the devastating justice Michael had meted out, Officer Morgan lost track for a moment. The battered young woman behind Richard seized the opportunity to retrieve Brown's gun and screamed in rage as she aimed wildly and fired.

Thankfully for Michael, she missed him by a good foot and a half. "Onion" wasn't so lucky because the errant bullet shattered his skull and sliced through his brain. Richard screamed, "Drop the gun!" but Brown's erstwhile lover tried to steady the gun and prepared to fire at Michael again. With no other choice, Richard aimed at the enraged woman and pulled the trigger. Demonstrating unusual restraint, he only fired once but it was center-mass as he'd been trained to do when facing a deadly threat and the slug punctured her heart.

No longer drunk with vengeance, Michael was stunned by the turn of events. He couldn't think or move. However, although Richard's heart was filled with remorse, his mind took over instantly. "Michael, get out of here!"

"But what about them? I didn't want there to be any more killing."

Richard tapped into every ounce of authority he possessed and commanded, "Leave! Now!"

Michael did as he was told. Richard didn't need to stage the scene before the other officers and police investigators arrived. The evidence matched up perfectly with the report he filed even though he left out one critical detail. Officer Morgan said he'd happened upon a domestic dispute and intervened to save the girl. Then he described how she'd turned on him during the violent, physical altercation when he tried to arrest the boyfriend. Only she missed when she shot at him and accidentally killed Brown. The ballistics fit as did her fingerprints on the gun and there was plenty of physical evidence to justify Morgan stepping in to rescue the girl.

By the time Richard was able to rehash the tragedy with Michael, the latter had shed the outward signs of remorse but remained deeply troubled. "I'm so sorry. All I wanted to do was teach the guy a lesson and have you put him away."

Richard tried not to throw salt in the wound, "I realize that, Michael, but these situations can get out of hand so easily." He gazed at Michael with sympathetic, caring eyes, "I'm a cop. We face this all the time." Michael looked at Richard with pitiful eyes seeking any kind of relief. "This is why I wanted you to leave the cop work to me." A bit of frustration flashed in Richard's eyes. "Why in the world did you follow me?"

"I wanted to help. I wanted to work together as a team."

This sparked some anger, "But you're not a cop!"

Michael reacted in kind, "I know but I sure as hell have a stake in this game."

"No, you don't! This is a police matter! Can't you get that through your thick skull?"

"I guess not! My brain is clogged up with bull crap!" Vengeance seemed to take over again. "Sally's wasting away like a vegetable and her attackers are being pampered by the so-called justice system." Michael caught himself before condemning the police.

Richard tried to reason with him, "Two attackers aren't being pampered."

With Sally still on his mind, Michael cruelly said, "Two down, two to go."

"I'll get the other two. I promise."

"Let me help you."

"Michael, I can't do that. You'll just have to trust me."

"But why?"

"After what just happened, I need to explain? Really?" Richard exhaled long and loud to regain his composure. "Look, what would have happened if Brown or his girlfriend had survived?" This seemed to sink in and Michael remained quiet. "Yeah, they would have put you at the scene, identified you and tied you to AA." Michael bowed his head in resignation. "And do you know what else? I would have been charged as an accessory-after-the-fact in Jenkins' death."

Michael responded apologetically, "Yeah, you're right."

Richard tried to put Michael's hunger for justice to bed for good with a bit of levity. "I might have to start calling you *Felix the Cat* instead of the Avenging Angel because you must have nine lives."

Michael retorted, "By my count, I still have six lives left."

Richard let it go as a harmless joke but should have worried. That's because Michael's heartfelt desire hadn't changed. He was still determined to see that Sally got justice, fully and fairly. However, he realized that he wouldn't be working with Officer Morgan as part of a dynamic duo. He still needed his help though because he didn't know where Darnell-Wright or Billups lived. Consequently, he continued to trail Richard as he patrolled. Only, this time, he kept his distance.

164

Morgan, true to his word, began stalking Casey Billups. It didn't take long for the cop to lead Michael to some of his favorite haunts. "Beast" was a big fella who liked to display his prowess on the basketball court. Once or twice a week, he could be found at a neighborhood playground where his thunderdunks were legendary. The trick for Michael was catching him there when Officer Morgan was busy elsewhere.

This approach presented a problem. By going it alone and staking out the playground, how could Michael catch "Beast" in the act of committing a crime? Even if he lucked out, how could he detain him long enough for Officer Morgan to come to the rescue and make the arrest? The devil was in the details but Michael wasn't about to get caught up in the weeds. He just wanted to get the guy.

There was another obstacle that escaped Michael's attention. Even though the media wasn't able to make any connection to AA, Billups and Darnell-Wright were suspicious of "Onion's" death. It took their already-heightened sense of awareness to a whole new level. With both of them on red alert, it wouldn't be easy for Michael or Richard to take either one by surprise.

Even if he had known, this wouldn't have deterred Michael who was hellbent for justice. He thought he had the perfect opportunity one evening as he watched the pick-up game from his car a safe distance away. Morgan was elsewhere and Billups and his pals didn't stop until darkness forced them to call it quits. Michael followed at a safe distance, dressed all in black with his hood up. One by one, his companions peeled off until Billups was all alone. Spying a dark alley up ahead, Michael closed the gap silently, snuck up behind the big man and shoved his pistol in his back. Michael whispered, "Turn right. Down the alley."

Billups froze, immovable as a mountain, "What you want with me?"

Michael was deadly serious, "Last chance. Get your fat ass down that alley if you want to live." Billups followed orders but moved as slow as molasses. About ten yards down the alleyway, Michael ordered, "Stop. Now, turnaround." Casey Billups showed no fear. Instead, he glared at Michael with a look of disdain. "Don't you recognize me?" Billups didn't change his expression so Michael pulled his mask down, "Now, do you recognize me?"

"Yeah, I remember yo punk ass, Karate Man." Billups sneered at the much smaller man. "I remember that fine lady of yours too."

Michael fought to ward off a knee-jerk reaction, "Shut your mouth!"

"Or what? What you gonna do, little man? Gonna shoot me?" The giant laughed in derision, "Go head then, pull the trigger."

Michael tried to counter with his own show of bravado. "Here's what we're going to do." Billups laughed with his hands placed confidently on his hips and casually let Michael finish. As he pulled out his phone, Michael explained, "I'm going to call the police. When they arrive, you're going to confess to what you did to my wife." Billups roared with laughter. Michael didn't blink an eye, "Then, you're going to rat on your pal Darnell-Wright."

With surprising quickness, the big man swung his arm and backhanded the phone out of Michael's hand. It crashed into the brick wall and dropped to the hard concrete below. Billups moved purposefully in that direction and stamped his heel down on the phone for good measure. "So much for that."

Michael pointed his gun and just stared back calmly in a way that Billups must have interpreted as cowardice. "Naw, you won't do it. Ain't got the balls." With that, Billups showed complete disrespect for Michael by calmly pulling a gun out of his pocket, slowly and methodically. His brazen disregard for his own safety proved totally foolish. Michael kicked the gun out of his hand before he could aim it.

"Beast" shrugged it off. "That ain't gone work, little man." He casually strolled over to pick up the gun.

"Don't do it! I'll shoot!" Casey Billups paid no attention and retrieved the gun anyway. As he turned back to face him, Michael dropped into a shooting crouch. Resolutely he cautioned, "This is your last chance."

Billups paid no heed and grabbed the top of his gun to load a cartridge into the chamber. Then he turned his hand palm down, gangster style, and aimed. Michael pulled the trigger and plugged the mountainous man right in the gut. Billups lost his grip on the gun and halted momentarily with an incredulous look on his face as if he couldn't believe Michael actually defended himself. Then blind rage possessed him and he lurched toward Michael looking like a mad grizzly on his hind legs. His hands clamped around Michael's neck like two meat hooks. Michael could not break free from the bellicose bull. As a last resort, he fired another round. It took three more to stop Billups from choking the life out of him.

By this time, windows started to open in the surrounding apartments. Thankfully for Michael, gunshots were not unusual in this hardcore neighborhood so, no one came out immediately to get a look at him. After taking a moment to catch his breath, Michael had the warped piece of mind to leave his calling card. Like in the past, he preferred *Duracell*, the copper top AA. He was able to make it back to his car without being followed. As he drove away, a twisted thought crossed his mind, *I wonder if I could be Duracell's new spokesman?*

Chapter 10:

The media was abuzz with news of the Avenging Angel's latest victim. They paid no attention to the fact that Casey Billups had been armed with a gun. No mention was made of his criminal record and violent past. They painted him as a gentle giant whose life had been snuffed out by the heartless vigilante, AA. They posted pictures of him from years before as an innocent-looking boy. The local news created an uproar against the police who, they claimed, were derelict in their duty to protect defenseless citizens like Casey Billups. His ominous nickname, "Beast" Billups, was never used. There were incessant calls for a full investigation.

Meanwhile, Michael Wyatt had to endure another lecture from Officer Richard Morgan. "I can't believe you did this again!"

Michael tried to defend himself, "I kept you out of it this time."

Morgan dug in his heels, "When are you going to realize, I'm up to my eyeballs in complicity – whether we're together or not!"

Michael didn't want to hear it, "Hey, go ahead and turn me in then. Anything to shut you up."

It was a wonder that Richard didn't cuss a blue streak. Instead, he silently counted to ten and tried to appeal to reason, "It's way too late for that now." This took the wind out of Michael's sails. "Even if I wanted to bail on you, I'd have a hell of a time explaining why I didn't stop you long before." Michael slumped in regretful shame. Richard noted the change of heart and tried to repair the bridge between them. "Besides, I'm on your side. We're all on your side."

"We're? Who's we're?"

"Just about every cop on the force."

"Did you tell the other cops about me?"

"Of course not. They don't know who you are but they've got eyes. The cops can see through the media's BS." This seemed to inflate Michael's sagging spirit. "You're a hero, man! They wish their hands weren't tied behind their backs by the City so they could do the same thing and bust these animals."

"What about you? Are you okay with it then?"

"Yeah, I feel the same way." Richard's smile disappeared as he offered this sober advice, "But you're still going about this the wrong way."

Michael tensed up as if ready to rebuke his cop pal but held his tongue. "You're asking for trouble."

"What could I have done differently? I tried to call you and he destroyed my phone. When I got the drop on him, he totally ignored me. Despite giving him several chances, he kept coming at me." Michael shook his head in disbelief, "I know I sound like a broken record but I had no choice. It was self-defense one-hundred percent."

"I get that. I'm not even going to badmouth you for being there in the first place. But why the battery?"

"It's my calling card. I wanted Darnell-Wright to know."

"And the media and the City?"

"Yeah, I guess I wasn't thinking in the heat of the moment."

"I'll say. Without that battery, it would have looked like a drug deal gone bad, gang payback or some such thing. Now, there's going to be incredible heat."

"Yeah, there's no doubt. But this will all blow over once I've finished with Darnell-Wright."

Richard was shocked by the callousness of Michael's response, "What are you smoking? You've got to stop this now!"

"Three down, one to go."

Richard tried to appeal to reason again. "Do you really think Sally would want this kind of retribution?"

Michael remained detached and retorted disdainfully, "If only she could tell me herself."

What Morgan couldn't accomplish, Darcy Darnell-Wright did. He shut down Michael Wyatt by going into his shell. The savvy thug was bound and determined not to end up like his three pals. The "King" curtailed every criminal activity that couldn't be carried out through surrogates. He made himself so scarce that even Officer Morgan couldn't get a sniff of his whereabouts. It was as if he'd vanished off the face of the earth.

Michael felt stranded and all alone. Sally was helpless to offer any real companionship and his only close friend, Richard, was busy with his duties as a cop. His work didn't occupy nearly enough of his time. Without his pursuit of Darnell-Wright to fill the void, Michael became like a caged animal. Somehow, he needed to let off some steam. Watching the news only added to his frustration. Rioting continued under the guise of peaceful protesting and the criminals got off scot free while the cops kept getting bashed.

The lunacy intensified as a couple of nationally prominent court cases wound down. Although they were far outside Missouri, St. Louis was impacted like most other urban centers across the country. It fanned the flames of the well-coordinated, ongoing unrest when grand juries failed to indict or juries issued acquittals. Never mind that there was clear evidence of self-defense that justified the use of deadly force by the cops in question. Likewise, no one seemed to care that prosecutors had been wildly overzealous in seeking premeditated, first-degree murder charges. The facts didn't matter since the mob demanded blind vengeance and the rabid media supported them whole hog.

As a result, places like Ferguson, Florissant and the City of St. Louis that were already beset with problems exploded with intensified arson, looting and violence. There was also a spate of new cop killings that were nothing short of premeditated assassinations. When one occurred in our town, Michael found new inspiration to occupy his time. Even if he couldn't track down Darnell-Wright, the Avenging Angel could still do his part to stand up for the police and silent majority who were under attack.

Michael Wyatt, dressed all in black like a modern-day ninja, roamed about skirting the melees in North City and County. With goggles and mask, he was able to blend in with the rioters. He learned to avoid any situation that might put him at odds with the mob or draw the attention of the ubiquitous media and cell phone cameras. Instead, he developed a great knack for identifying vulnerable malefactors and luring them off into the shadows where he could mete out his own form of frontier justice.

Michael made quite an impact without killing anyone. Although there were no dead bodies, he produced plenty of evidence to burnish the legend of the Avenging Angel. Concussions, blackened eyes, bloodied noses, broken bones and battered bodies were left in his wake for the authorities to retrieve. Each was accompanied by his now infamous calling card. The AA batteries could have been emblazoned with this motto: Have Mad Skills – Will Kick Butt. Although they denounced him, the local media ate it up. AA was great for ratings.

It wasn't surprising that the national media picked up on the story too. They gave it much the same spin saying that a crazed vigilante was preying on innocent protesters in the Gateway City. Their aim, besides garnering ratings gold, was to paint AA as exhibit one pointing to the right's true nature as violent, bigoted and hateful. Much to their chagrin, their narrative produced unintended consequences in some circles. A few folks began to see AA as a heroic figure, especially among law enforcement. More importantly though, tales of the Avenging Angel sent a chill through the ranks of the unruly mobs. Where would AA strike next in St. Louis? Would he or copycats spring up elsewhere? With the cops defanged and corrupt prosecutors, mayors and governors on their side, they'd been able to brazenly spread their anarchy. Did they now have to proceed with caution, watching their backs constantly?

The black *Dirty Harry* didn't have much to say to his crime-fighting friend. Not only did he know it was useless to try to stop Michael but, in truth, he was part of the growing minority who saw AA as a hero. Besides, he figured that these random acts would help draw attention away from AA's true identity since they provided no link to Michael's crusade against Darnell-Wright and his former crew. Rather than being troubled by AA's vigilantism, it bothered Richard much more to hear the media's spin. It ticked him off to no end to see the way they rushed to the defense of the thugs while ignoring the deaths of his brothers and sisters in blue who'd lost their lives in the ongoing war on cops.

Unfortunately, Richard let his enthusiasm get in the way of better judgment. He became way too vocal among his cop peers in expressing his support for the Avenging Angel. Every barrel had its rotten apples and the cops were no different. There was a mole among the ranks who fed inside information back to the prosecutor's office. They, in turn, cast Officer Richard Morgan as a rabble rouser. At first, it only resulted in veiled punishments like being assigned to lousy beats and odd shifts. However, Richard got the message: watch your step, mister!

Something else happened to dampen his enthusiasm for AA's clandestine crusade. Death at the hands of AA had taken a holiday but it returned with a vengeance. That's because the wary anarchists went to school on the Avenging Angel. Although the media tried to portray the so-called peaceful protests as somehow organic, populist uprisings, the truth was vastly different. Groups like Antifa and BLM were well-funded and highly organized. Their leadership met and strategized regularly and they gathered intelligence to guide their battle plans.

They recognized the Avenging Angel as a threat on multiple levels. He not only represented a physical danger to their members but an ideological hazard that had to be strangled in the cradle. The last thing they needed was some everyman anti-hero stirring the silent majority to rise up from their slumber and fear. He needed to be culled out and eliminated. The only question was how?

In studying the various incidents where AA had left his calling card, they recognized a clear pattern. The Avenging Angel looked like one of them and moved about undetected. Somehow, he'd lured an unsuspecting few away from the safety of the crowds before striking. They surmised correctly that he was too smart to give himself away in situations where the numbers didn't favor him. Thus, they'd have to draw him out to where he'd feel safe.

Theirs was a clever, well thought out plan designed to make the hunter the hunted. Since he always struck at night during the riots, they assigned hit squads to each event. Small groups of three people were instructed to lay in wait around the fringes and allow themselves to be drawn away. However, knowing AA's M. O., they wouldn't be caught unawares. They'd be armed to the teeth and trained to handle the types of confrontations that had doomed their cohorts.

Michael Wyatt, unaware of the plot against him, continued to wage a private war on the anarchists by peeling away unsuspecting members of the mobs. Twice more he was able to succeed in pummeling thugs and leaving them for the police with his calling card left behind. Little did he know that his pursuers were closing in, using this latest intelligence to tighten the invisible noose surrounding him.

The third time was the charm for the nefarious ambushers. The three-man squad looked ripe for the picking, hanging at the edge of the melee and chanting and cheering while leaving the heavy lifting to other thugs closer to the action. Michael approached them urgently as if he were winded and claimed he needed their help. They seemed willing enough so, he told them a breathless tale of how he'd found a couple of Trump supporters spying on them down the block. He added that they were taking video of the riots and needed to be stopped.

They followed Michael at a trot while vowing to make the white supremacists pay dearly.

Michael couldn't help but be amused by the fact that one of the three was a woke white guy. This had almost become routine for Michael so, he never suspected that he was putting himself in danger by luring them away from the crowd, cameras and witnesses. When they arrived at a deserted parking lot that was hidden behind an empty building, one of the three asked, "So, where are they?"

Michael went into the same dialogue that had shocked the other thugs he'd dispatched in similar situations. He spoke in a matter-of-fact, almost snide tone of voice. "Gentlemen, I'm sorry to disappoint you but there are no Trump supporters to beat up. I lied. However, if you need to work out your frustration, I guess you can try to pummel me." Normally, this would lead to perplexed looks and debilitating confusion.

However, these guys were different. One said, "Really?" as all three moved slowly in choreographed fashion. One took up a position directly in front of Michael while the other stood behind him with the third creeping up to his left side.

Michael was already in the process of dropping the bomb. "Yes, really. But I must caution you against any violence. You see, I'm the type that will fight back." He brandished a battery to put the fear of God into them but they seemed oddly unaffected. Michael shrugged and continued, "Here's what we're going to do. I'm going to call the police and, if you cooperate, you'll be arrested and spend some time in jail."

"And if we don't cooperate?"

"Then it's on you as to what happens next."

Simultaneously, the three savvy thugs produced weapons. The guy in front pointed a handgun at Michael's chest while the man behind him positioned a knife close to his back. The big guy on his left, slipped on some brass knuckles. Apparently, they wanted to administer a good beating before taking Michael's life. The front man issued this order, "Give me your phone and wallet."

Michael put his hands up in surrender, "Okay fellas, I don't want any trouble." Looking extremely nervous as he grabbed his phone and wallet, Michael seemed to fidget, looking backwards at the deadly blade. He compliantly set the phone and wallet down on the ground, "Please don't hurt me. I have a wife."

The man behind the gun sneered, "The great Avenging Angel! You don't sound so tough now, do you?"

Michael whimpered, "Please, just let me go. I won't ever bother you or your friends again. I promise." Although he sounded pitiful and cowardly, there was a method to his madness. While play acting, Michael was carefully taking stock of the situation. He gauged the distance between his right hand and the gun while noting that the knife was in the other thug's right hand positioned toward his right rib cage. He paid little attention to the brass knuckles which didn't pose an immediate threat.

The gunman was all business, "Now, take out your gun." Michael knew it was useless to deny that he had a gun. "And slowly!" He reached inside his hoodie and pulled his gun out gingerly between his thumb and forefinger, butt first. "That's right." Michael stooped down cautiously and set the Glock on the ground.

"Take my money. Take my phone. Please, just don't hurt me."

"Before we get on with business, hand me that wallet," he motioned to the big fella. "I wanna share your name with everyone, Mr. Avenging Angel." Turning again to the hulking

182

thug off to Michael's left, "Hand me his phone too. I want to record this for everyone to see."

Michael knew what was coming next so, he threw them for a loop by asking nonsensically, "What time is it?"

This had the desired effect of breaking their train of thought, "What the?"

Michael sprang into action with the precision of a Swiss watch. He swung the heel of his right hand in a laser arc, striking the gunman's wrist hard enough to collapse his hand inward. Within a millisecond, he brought his left hand forward with his right and twisted the gun backwards, taking it away from the startled thug. While using his arms thusly, he'd stepped his right foot over the left and tucked in his ribs. The knife was thrust into thin air just off to his right side. Michael dropped his right elbow and pinned the blade against his side.

With his feet crossed, Michael pirouetted like a prima ballerina and slammed his left elbow into the skull of the thug behind him while maintaining his grip on the gun. The knife clanged against the pavement. The big man with the brass knuckles was much too slow. Michael easily dodged his sweeping hook and backed away to a safe distance. "Don't move!"

Like a complete fool, the guy who'd lost his gun to Michael didn't heed Michael's warning. Maybe he was conditioned to think he was invulnerable because the cops had backed down from him on numerous occasions and he'd been released the next day after the few times he'd been arrested. Maybe he was still under the spell of Michael's feigned cowardice even after his martial arts display. In any case, he seemed oblivious to the danger when he bent down, picked up Michael's gun and prepared to fire.

Michael screamed, "Nooooooo!" as he reflexively defended himself but his frantic plea was drowned out by the gun's loud report. The other two animals still showed no fear as one grabbed the knife and the big man's wide eyes burned with pure rage. Michael fired another round into the sky and lowered the gun with deadly determination on his face, "One more step and you're dead!" They halted and Michael cautiously retrieved his phone. As he dialed 911 to summon the police, the two thugs turned and walked away; slowly at first and then more briskly.

Michael vowed, "Stop or I'll shoot!" but they correctly calculated that he wouldn't kill again.

When they were out of range, the big man turned and screamed, "We'll get you!"

Michael was overcome with remorse, not that he had let them escape justice but that he'd been forced to kill another person to defend his own life. The gunman had surely deserved his fate but that didn't ease his guilt. Taking a man's life under any circumstances was tragic and heartrending. That's why, even if it meant being captured, he wouldn't have killed the two men as they walked away. He didn't have it in him. Only after reflecting on the situation later did he realize that his identity was still safe. They hadn't removed his mask or had time to look through his wallet or phone.

Chapter 11:

He expected a call from Richard as the media trumpeted their outrage against the mystery-man they considered a vile vigilante. This time, Michael didn't leave a copper top battery behind but the two escaped thugs reported that the killer had proudly displayed his signature calling card while attacking them. He was perplexed as he left for work the next day. *Surely, Richard was aware of the killing.*

Still, no word came from his cop pal. That is, until Michael took a stroll downtown at lunchtime to grab some fast food several blocks away from the office building where he worked. From behind he heard, "Pssst, follow me." He turned and saw someone heading into the alleyway. As he followed the man, he saw the back of a cop's uniform. Once they were far enough away from the crowded sidewalk, Richard turned to face him.

"Why so secret?"

Richard seemed uncharacteristically nervous. "I gotta make this quick. Can't be seen with you."

"What the heck?"

"Just shut up and listen," he whispered. Richard's serious demeanor demanded Michael's silence. "Somebody on the force ratted me out. The heat's really on this time."

This shocked Michael, "Do they know about us?"

"Thankfully, no – but we've gotta keep it that way. They're all over me, watching my every move. I can't be seen with you. Can't leave a phone record, nothing." Michael nodded with his eyes wide in amazement. "Get rid of your phone. Buy a new one and change the number. If you need to reach me in a pinch, use one of those burner phones that can't be traced and buy it with cash."

Dumbfounded, Michael asked nervously, "You're my only real friend. Will I ever see you again?"

Richard tried to sound reassuring, "Of course but, for the time being, we've got to lay low." Michael slumped. "Don't worry. I'll be in touch. Just no calls from your personal phone and I can't come by your place or Sally's room." Michael stared with a quizzical look. "I'll find you. Don't worry."

Michael couldn't eat. He went back to work but his mind was elsewhere. When he got home that evening, he was gripped with such anxiety that he broke out in a cold sweat. He realized he'd been set up and would have to stop preying on the rioters to avoid falling into another trap. His prime motivation, seeking justice for Sally, was lost when Darnell-Wright vanished into thin air. His visits to see Sally left him feeling hopeless and helpless. Now, to top it all off, he was all but cut off from his only real friend and confidant.

Michael was too much of a fitness freak to drown his sorrows in booze. Even classic movies couldn't take his mind off of the claustrophobic loneliness he felt. Kicking up his running, lifting and martial arts workouts to new heights helped him sleep better through exhaustion but didn't soothe his nagging feelings of uselessness and abandonment. Since he trained alone, Michael couldn't objectively gauge his karate skills. Little did he know that his prowess, already considerable, was jumping to freakish new heights as a result of his almost-compulsive, solitary regimen. It would come in handy later.

At his wit's end, a crazy idea crept into his head. It was ludicrous but, in his current state, seemed fully arrayed in sanity. *Why not take the show on the road? Weekends were the worst so, why not get away?* There were fertile fields abounding where the Avenging Angel could reap his harvest: Chicago, Portland, Seattle, Louisville and New York just to name a few.

Unfortunately, due to their odd new circumstances, Richard wasn't there to serve as the voice of reason. Michael's conscience was no help either. In solitude, there was no one to challenge his logic. He never even considered whether it was just and right to carry on with his personal war against lawless thugs and anarchists. In his mind, there was no choice but to stand up for the forgotten men and women who'd been abandoned by the proper authorities charged with ensuring their safety.

Instead, he drifted off to tactical renderings. He wondered where he should go outside of St. Louis. Flying could leave a paper trail. On the other hand, driving would limit him to a range of mileage that would put St. Louis in the center. After careful consideration, Michael decided a mixture would provide the best cover. He could drive to Chicago, Kansas City or Louisville for the weekend without missing any work. In between, he'd target New York, Portland or Seattle but avoid direct flights. For example, he could jet to Philly or Baltimore and drive from there into NYC.

Michael would be stocked with ample cash. There'd be no overnight stays or credit card purchases in any of his final destinations. Twist and shout, in and out. He even went so far as to dream up elaborate justifications for longer trips requiring air travel. He'd always wanted to climb the museum steps in Philly like *Rocky Balboa*. This was far-fetched but he was thinking ahead. If some dedicated, smart investigator was ever able to connect the dots pointing to him, he'd be prepared with a ready explanation. Like with scaling the walls at Sally's medical center, Michael was prepared to go to any lengths to conceal his identity while battling the forces of evil.

Richard would have told him in no uncertain terms that going nationwide would only turn up the heat further and place him in greater jeopardy. However, Michael was of a vastly different mindset. Without Sally's thoughtful influence and Richard's practical guidance, he behaved like a wild stallion. In some respects, his alter ego took over. He actually saw himself, first and foremost, as a crusading crime fighter. Move over *Bruce Wayne* and *Clark Kent*. At times, Michael Wyatt gave way to the Avenging Angel. It gave him purpose and drive.

His first venture out of the St. Louis metropolitan area led him to Chicago's South Side. It was an easy, five-hour drive and more than ripe for AA's old west form of justice. Every weekend was a lawless thug-fest so, targets were plentiful. Michael didn't need to worry about falling into a trap. Although elements of BLM and Antifa were well-connected to organizers who pulled the strings in other cities across the country, no one was on the lookout for the Avenging Angel outside of St. Louis.

It proved easy for Michael to lure two unsuspecting victims away from one of the teeming mobs. Thereafter, he had his routine down pat with one added twist. Michael opened his soliloquy with this discombobulating question, "Ever hear of the Avenging Angel?" He waved a battery in front of them for good measure.

The startled pair's jaws dropped. One responded in disbelief, "Crazy dude from the Lou?"

AA cast a sinister smile, nodded and replied, "Road trip." Then he pulled out his Glock to beat them to the punch. He'd heard all about the rampant gun violence in Chicago and didn't want to let them get the drop on him. Behind another disturbing grin, "Or maybe I'm just a copycat." The two thugs cast desperate, bewildered looks toward one another. "Take out your guns slowly – by the barrels and toss them over here." They hesitated slightly and AA crouched in a shooting stance, "Don't make me shoot."

Something in his deadly demeanor convinced them to comply. "What'd we ever do to you, man?"

They had to be bothered by his nonchalance, "Me personally? Nothing." But then his tone struck a hard edge, "It's what you've done to my people."

"Your people? Who in the hell are your people?"

The rising anger in the thug's voice didn't rattle Michael one iota. "They're all of the law-abiding citizens out there who are just trying to make ends meet without the likes of you disrupting their lives. They don't ask for much. Just a little peace, safety and – freedom."

"You crazy."

"Maybe I am. But you're crazy if you think no one's going to fight back."

Anger rose as pure hatred shot from the thug's eyes, "What you gone do?"

Michael kicked their guns away a safe distance and stared eerily. He looked like a starving man glaring at a juicy ribeye. "The choice is yours."

"What the?"

"Here's the deal. I'm going to call Chicago's finest. You can deal with them – or take your chances with me."

They both laughed as if they'd been let off the hook. "You against the two of us?"

"Yep."

"What about the gun?" Michael tossed his Glock over by their handguns. They cut loose with more husky laughter. "You on, fool!"

They both produced knives but it didn't faze Michael. He would have let them off with a good beating but instead left both of them with broken wrists as he disarmed his shocked opponents. When he took out his burner phone and contacted the police, they attempted to run. For their efforts, they were rewarded with disabling knee injuries. With his work done and the sirens drawing near, Michael took his leave after gracing them with his calling card. For his first out-of-town venture, he left a special gift. After blowing up the twelve-inch, plastic, inflatable Duracell, he fitted it with a pair of paper wings.

Buoyed by success, Michael decided to take a victory lap of sorts by cruising through the neighborhood before heading home. He was motivated partly by curiosity. *Could the South Side really be as bad as they made it out to be on Fox News?* Every weekend the astounding death toll from gun violence went higher and higher.

It didn't take long for him to see living proof. A wild party had spilled out into the streets. Michael pulled over to observe the raucous revelry from a safe distance. A short time later, a car rolled up to the party from the other direction and the lone gunman opened fire indiscriminately. Several people fell to the ground, wounded or dead. One errant bullet shattered a window in a nearby apartment and a frantic woman screamed from the balcony, "My baby!"

Michael ducked down and watched in secret as the killer sped by him. With total disregard for his own well-being, Michael went after the speeding vehicle. When the shooter saw that he was being chased, he became even more reckless in attempting to escape. Michael figured that the fleeing felon probably feared that a rival gang member was in hot pursuit. The Avenging Angel gave nary a thought to what might happen to him if he cornered the dangerous thug or, worse, the police showed up to catch him in the act.

Any chance of reflecting on his reckless behavior disappeared when the marauding killer turned too sharply, caught a curb and reeled uncontrollably on two wheels before careening into a parked car. Somehow, despite the thunderous, metal-crunching impact, the perp climbed from the car and scurried away toward the darkness with a stilted hitch in his gait. Michael followed in his car to pursue the killer and move his vehicle away from the scene of the crash. Several blocks away, the hobbled thug turned right down a dark alleyway.

Michael parked and chased after him on foot. Halfway down the lonely corridor, the perp was blocked by a ten-foot chain link fence topped by barbed wire. After a couple of futile attempts to climb with his bum knee, the man turned to face his pursuer with his gun drawn. Michael ducked behind a trash dumpster, pulled out his Glock and warned, "Drop it or I'll shoot!" The man reacted without thinking, like a cornered rat, and began firing wildly in Michael's direction. One slug ricocheted off the brick wall behind the dumpster and caught Michael in his right side.

His gunshot wound brought back terrible memories of a bout with a kidney stone as the white-hot, searing pain caused Michael to double over. Unhinged by fear and hatred, the gunman popped another clip into his pistol and fired toward the dumpster as he made a mad dash to exit the alley. Michael fought through the pain, hit the deck and rolled from behind his cover with his arms out and both hands on the Glock. He was able to maintain his calm and focus despite the hail of bullets buzzing all around him. He squeezed the trigger slowly and launched the deadly lead missile. It hit home with such force that it knocked the man sideways.

Michael approached cautiously, ready to shoot again, if necessary. The man was still alive but couldn't speak. Blood was gurgling from his mouth. His face was filled with terror as one who faced the grim reaper without any prospects for the afterlife but doom. "I'm sorry. I'll call for help." Michael dialed 911 and explained that he'd just made a citizen's arrest of a gangster who'd shot up a street party and likely injured an innocent baby in the process. "I had to shoot the man in self-defense."

"What is your location?"

Michael described it as best he could. "He's badly hurt and needs help right away. Please send an ambulance."

"Yes sir. What is your name?"

"Never mind that. Just get someone here as quickly as possible!"

"Please stay where you are. I've just dispatched a cruiser. The police should arrive shortly. An ambulance will follow."

Michael could hear the sirens in the distance. He hung up the phone and looked sympathetically at the man's trembling face. "Hang on. Help is on the way." After turning to leave, Michael stopped. "Your life is in God's hands. Now is the time to repent. Tell God you're sorry and ask for His forgiveness in Jesus' name. God will surely forgive you." Michael reached into his hoodie to leave his calling card but, when he looked into the poor man's eyes, buried the battery back in his pocket. His last words were, "I'll pray for you," before he made his getaway.

AA made a beeline for home. Running on pure adrenaline, he didn't notice the pain until the white dashes blurred by him on the highway.

When he reached down to inspect, the blood was thick and sticky like someone had spilled a bunch of red syrup. Michael worked up the courage to press along the full length of the seven-inch wound. As he probed gingerly, he was relieved to find no slug buried in his flesh. Apparently, the bullet had passed clean through in a non-vital area where most men his age had ample love handles. Still, it throbbed and hurt like hell.

Instinct told him to stop for first-aid supplies to clean and bind the wound but he didn't want to risk drawing attention. Instead, Michael removed his hoodie, wadded it up, and pressed it against his side to stop the bleeding. It was a long ride home which gave him plenty of time to think. The euphoria he'd felt after dispatching the two anarchists was long forgotten. Now, he was haunted by the terrified look on the wounded man's face. As promised, he prayed for the man; not only his physical recovery but a spiritual transformation.

Overcome by guilt and a sickening sense that he'd taken his personal crusade much too far, Michael turned on the radio to try to create a mind-numbing diversion. He wanted some ear-splitting music to distract his troubled conscience but, within minutes, the local media cut in with breaking news about another shooting. His worst fears were confirmed. The crazed gunman had shot and killed a little baby girl sleeping in her crib. This should have provided all the justification he needed but it still didn't soothe his troubled soul.

Once the word got out that the infamous Avenging Angel had struck outside of St. Louis, there was a media feeding-frenzy. National outlets rushed to interview the two survivors from their hospital beds. According to the reporters, two peaceful protesters were the victims of an unprovoked attack by a white man dressed in black who claimed to be St. Louis' Avenging Angel. One bedridden thug exclaimed, "Yeah, he flashed one of those little batteries in front of us.

His partner in crime clarified, "But he said he might be a copycat."

The first man added, "He left this souvenir," as he proudly displayed the inflatable Duracell with the paper wings attached.

The media had a field day with this conundrum. Speculation abounded. Had the Avenging Angel expanded his hunting grounds beyond St. Louis? Or was it possible that he'd inspired another sick individual to mimic his dreadful deeds in the Windy City? It was duly noted that AA had never before used an inflatable battery as his calling card. One reporter really tried to fan the flames with this question, "Could this give rise to a broader movement across the country? What if this was the work of a white supremacist network?" Of course, this notion came full circle when the reporter implied that President Trump may have inspired the obviously racist conspiracy.

The other shooting almost went unnoticed since gangland violence was so commonplace. However, by chance, the baby killer wound up in the same hospital where the two thugs were being treated. One savvy reporter noticed the police presence around the gunshot victim and began asking questions. One thing led to another and the press discovered that the third victim had been shot by a man fitting the description of the Avenging Angel or his copycat.

It didn't take long for the media to begin issuing dire warnings that a maniac was loose on the streets of Chicago. Sadly, no one seemed to care about the tragic death of the baby girl. That part of the story was swept under the rug. When the shooter was out of surgery and finally able to address the press, he noted, "Dude was crazy. He kept talking about God. Said he was going to pray for me – after shooting me. Crazy!" This gave the press license to brand the Avenging Angel as a religious fanatic on top of being a racist. If there was anything good that came out of AA's trip to Chicago, it was that the media's fearmongering put a chill into the local gangs that tamped down on some of the gun violence, at least temporarily.

Part Three:

Captain Bucco

"Follow the money."

(DEEP THROAT IN ALL THE PRESIDENT'S MEN)

Chapter 12:

Michael disposed of the burner phone before
leaving Chicago. He didn't want there to be
anything to connect him to what had happened
there. His best hope was that the press would feed
the notion that a copycat had sprung up
elsewhere. When he got back into town, he
purchased another disposable phone but hesitated
to call Richard Morgan. He desperately needed to
talk to someone he could trust but debated
whether he should bring his cop pal into the loop
about Chicago. He'd already put him in hot water
with his St. Louis deeds and didn't want to make
matters worse for Richard.

Before he could resolve this dilemma,
Richard rendered the point moot. Michael found a
letter in the mail with no return address. When he
opened the envelope, there was a single piece of
paper with a one-line, typed message, "Meet me
at the bottom of Art Hill at 10:00 tonight." He
didn't need to be told to shred it. Michael was
nervous about revealing his latest exploits but
eagerly anticipated seeing his trusted friend.

In the meantime, I'd already latched onto the
news out of Chicago but had a different take than
the rest of my peers in the media. I reacted
joyously at the prospect that AA's backlash was

catching on elsewhere. While I knew this would draw scathing criticisms, it didn't matter. Rather than pulling back on the throttle, I juxtaposed the senseless rioting and anarchy against what I hailed as righteous anger on the part of the Avenging Angel and his potential acolytes in other cities.

Trying my best to reveal the true motivations behind the nationwide spate of so-called peaceful protests, I unleashed a merciless harangue on my radio show. As normal, I opened with my signature theme song, *Now You're Messing with a (Son of a Bitch)* by Nazareth. "A good Monday morning to all of you American patriots out there! Welcome to the only show where you get the truth, the whole truth and nothing but the truth. I'm your unhinged host, 'Rambo' Rooney."

I took some routine shots at the mainstream media whom I'd labeled as the enemy of the people long before President Trump coined the term fake news. Then I repeated my regular refrain that liberals were mentally ill before emphasizing that the party of John F. Kennedy had been overrun by 'Sandy' Cortez and 'Bolshevik' Bernie, as I called them. "It's not your grandfather's Democrat Party anymore. Heck, it's not your father's Democrat Party!"

With those salvos out of the way, I launched into my opening monologue. "How long have these quote/unquote peaceful protests been going on? Three months, four months? It's ridiculous if you ask me. I know some professional athletes whose careers haven't lasted that long. Good grief!" I paused just long enough to focus the audience's attention. "Does anybody remember George Floyd? I do but, for the most part, he seems to be a ghost of the past. Yeah, his death was a tragedy, no doubt. But was he really a hero?"

Never answer a question you can't answer yourself. "Let me remind you. The guy was a convicted felon who did hard time. He had a rap sheet as long as Pinocchio's nose. For crying out loud, he robbed a pregnant woman while holding a gun to her bulging stomach! Plus, we know now that he couldn't breathe before that worthless excuse of a cop ever touched him. Floyd had enough fentanyl in his system to kill a moose! But I digress."

I was on a roll. "Here's the key takeaway. Maybe, at first, the protests were peaceful and justified on some level. But they were hijacked, people! Do you really think these three or four months of sheer, nonstop anarchy across our entire country have been about social justice, whatever that means? Really? If you do, then I've got some swamp land in Florida I'd like to sell you."

I morphed into teacher-mode. "What have I told you forever? Whenever you're trying to figure out a mystery or uncover a scandal, all together class, FOLLOW THE MONEY!" I paused to let this sink in. "As I've said before, I can't take credit for this pearl of wisdom. It was made famous during Nixon's Watergate scandal when an informant known only as *Deep Throat* told Woodward and Bernstein to follow the money."

I couldn't hold back a good belly laugh. "Excuse me for laughing but I couldn't help it. That's because the Watergate break-in used to be considered the worst political scandal in American history," I huffed with disdain. "Russia-Gate makes Watergate look like child's play. And that even pales in comparison to what's going on right now." After a sobering pause, I concluded, "But the old adage still applies. FOLLOW THE MONEY."

Sounding professorial, I continued, "Pray tell, who's been paying the bills for the past three or four months? I mean, these people obviously aren't holding down steady jobs. And who's been paying for their food, transportation and supplies? It takes a lot of money to stage a good riot. The mobs need bricks, bottles, gasoline, bats, goggles, lasers, pepper spray and signage. These things don't grow on trees! Well, the bats kind of do." My producer played a cut from *All the President's Men* where *Deep Throat* furtively whispered his famous line. "That's right, class, follow the money." Since our younger listeners probably hadn't heard of the old Redford and Hoffmann flick, my trusty producer came back with Cuba Gooding Jr's famous line from *Jerry McGuire*. I mimicked it for good measure, "SHOW ME THE MONEY!" I ranted.

"Here's a clue for you, class. We have a pretty good idea who has been funding the campaigns of the shady prosecutors who were put in place in our major cities in the last election cycle. Happened right here in St. Louis too. Yeah, I'm talking about your favorite billionaire who disdains capitalism even though it's made him filthy rich. And I do mean rich. He's richer than Richie Richingstein." After another pause for effect, "And do you know which political party has been exclusively on the receiving end of his largesse? Yes class, altogether now, the Democrats. Or should I say Demon-Rats? And by the way, he's given oodles to BLM and Antifa too."

I challenged accusatorily like a trial lawyer, "Who has raised and donated tons of money to bail out the anarchists who've been arrested? Yes, the Democrats, Hollywood and members of the mainstream media. Even their VP candidate raised money to keep these criminals on the street." With perfect timing, my producer cut in with Boy George singing *Karma Chameleon*. "Yep, Kama-Kama-Kama-Kama-Kama-Kamaleon." I couldn't help but giggle at my own silliness.

However, I shifted to a serious tone to drive to the goal line. "If you follow the money, there's only one conclusion to be drawn." After another intentional pause, "The Democrats are behind the anarchy. It's all about politics folks. It's an election year! They still haven't accepted the results of the 2016 election and will do anything to win in 2020. And I do mean ANYTHING! Did I say anything? Think back over the past four years. We had a never-ending litany of Russia-Russia-Russia, the Kavanaugh debacle, bimbos, tax returns, Ukraine, the impeachment hoax and endless investigations and hearings."

I posited, "They weren't kidding when they said, 'Never let a crisis go to waste.' Is anyone else sick of Schiff-for-Brains? When they've run out of new lies and hoaxes, they've simply followed the instructions on their shampoo bottle: rinse and repeat. The sad thing is that, during all these so-called investigations, they never even attempted to get at the truth. Robert Mueller spent forty-million-dollars, that is, our hard-earned tax dollars, and didn't even mention the fraud committed against the FISA Court even though it was right under his nose. The fix is in, folks," I declared with finality.

"Now, some of you may be asking, 'Rooney, what's their motivation?' and that would be a valid point. Let me lay it out for you as simply as possible: power. It's all about money and power. Follow the money and it will lead you right to the culprits who are so power-hungry they'll stop at nothing to win the election."

I switched gears to make my case one more time before moving on to the next topic. "Have you noticed a change just recently as the election has drawn near? Yeah, we're not hearing as much about riots anymore. Why is that? Did they run out of money? No. Did the so-called organic protests suddenly run out of steam? No." I could almost see the ears leaning closer to their radios as I paused once more. "Look at the polls; the internal ones, not the fake ones. When the President started pounding the issue of law and order, the internal polls shifted. It became a political loser for the Democrats and, magically, the violence abated." I instinctively waved a magic wand even though the audience couldn't see me.

"It's no different than when Biden and Harris suddenly flip-flopped from their radical positions on fracking and fossil fuels. They will say and do whatever is convenient at the time and the media gives them a free pass." I cut loose with a sarcastic cackle. "They're between a rock and a hard place now. Their radical base is about to revolt over this sudden shift to the middle. The crazies are issuing new manifestos and pressing 'Trojan Horse' Biden and 'Comrade' Harris to get back in line."

At this point, I was unaware of the particulars involving AA's personal nemeses, Darnell-Wright and company, and how they'd used the riots as a backdrop to boost their own criminal endeavors. Yet, I could surmise as much from general observations. "And have you noticed that they haven't been able to stop the violence in our streets completely? It's hard to control the pestilence once you've opened Pandora's Box.

Sure, you can cut off their funding but the mob has a mind of its own and other sources of revenue like looting and extortion. BLM has scored millions upon millions by shaking down big corporations."

I gave my listeners a moment to reflect, "Speaking of BLM and Antifa, have you ever heard Biden, Harris or any top Dems denounce them? The President has been peppered over and over about white supremacists despite disavowing them many times. And where are all of these dreaded white supremacists? Have you seen them rioting and taking over whole sections of major cities? Have they burned down any police headquarters?" I laughed in derision.

"So, where does this leave us? I submit to you that most right-thinking, patriotic Americans have had just about enough. Yeah, we're pissed. But most of us are too afraid or law-abiding, maybe compliant would be a better word, to take a stand. Not the Avenging Angel though. Folks, he's not a pox as the media would have you believe. AA is a true hero! He is taking a stand for you and me: the silent majority. AA is personally putting into action what you and I would love to do. So, if there are copycats springing up outside of St. Louis, I say, AMEN!"

After going to commercial, my producer spoke excitedly in my headphones, "We've got a live one on line one. Says he's the Avenging Angel."

"Oh boy, here we go." I was used to getting crank callers. Unlike other talk shows, I let everyone have their turn on the air as long as they didn't use foul language or launch personal attacks. I felt like, the crazier the better. The audience loved it. "What does it say on caller ID?"

"Just unknown caller. Not even a phone number. Must be one of those prepaid phones."

"Oh well – no guts, no glory. I'll introduce him right after the break." I was mentally ready for some lunacy and tried to prepare our listeners with my best tongue-in-cheek intro. "We have a real treat for you, our loyal listeners. Usually, I like to give advance notice when interviewing a major celebrity but, in this case, we have an impromptu caller that I know you'll want to hear from. Without further ado, I'm pleased to bring you a real hero for our time; the man who has been dominating the news cycle for many weeks – drum roll please – none other than the one, the only, Avenging Angel!" My producer provided the perfect sound effects as if a crowd of thousands was applauding wildly.

"Welcome to the show. What should I call you, Avenging Angel, Mr. Angel, Ang?"

Usually, crank callers would play along with the gag. There was one guy who liked to say he was calling from Paris and spoke in a hilariously contrived French accent. Once, a pair of jokers called in as "Nature Boy" Ric Flair having a conversation with Randy "Macho Man" Savage from beyond the grave. They did a pretty good job with the woooooooos and oh yeaaaahhs. At first, I was greatly disappointed that this guy played it boringly straight and deadpanned, "You can call be AA for short."

I cut the comedy and said sarcastically, "Okay," drawing out the second syllable three times longer than the first. This gave me a moment to think on my feet. "So, to what do we owe this great honor?"

"I was just listening to your opening monologue and wanted to thank you."

"Really, why's that?"

"You're the only guy in this town; actually, you're the only person in the media anywhere, who's giving me a fair shake."

The guy sounded dead serious so, I tried a different approach and played it straight. "So, this is actually the Avenging Angel?"

"That's right."

"Okay, don't take this the wrong way but I'm sure you can understand how some people out there might think you're an imposter. It wouldn't be the first time we've had crank callers on the air."

"I understand completely."

"Then you won't mind if I ask you a few questions to verify the authenticity of this call?"

"Not at all."

"Well then. Tell me, how did you decide to start leaving AA batteries as your calling card?"

"It was actually an accident. I didn't mean to leave them behind the first time. When I used my homemade slapper to defend myself, some batteries fell out after it hit the ground."

"And where did this happen?"

"The downtown parking garage off Market."

"So that was you?"

"Yes."

"Why did you attack those men?"

The caller answered forcefully, "I did NOT attack those men. Those thugs attacked me. It was self-defense."

"Okay. Okay. I hear you. Why did you start leaving Duracell batteries thereafter?"

"I kind of liked the notoriety. Frankly, I hoped it would put the fear of God into the predators out there on the streets."

"What do you think of the name Avenging Angel?"

"Actually, I'm rather fond of it. At least, I liked the way you came up with it."

This pleasantly surprised me, "Thank you for giving me the credit. Most people think one of the local news sheeple came up with your moniker."

"We know better, don't we?" He snickered ever so slightly showing the first sign of having any sense of humor. "I'm a long-time listener 'Rambo' so, let's give credit where credit is due.

However, I'm not wild about the way the media has twisted it around to make me look like some kind of crazed vigilante."

"But aren't you taking the law into your own hands?"

"I know you're doing your job playing devil's advocate but, again, I'm a long-time listener. I know where you stand." This shut me up and I sat stunned while he continued. "You understand my motivation. I'm not seeking vengeance. I'm standing up for the silent majority; all the helpless folks who think enough is enough. When our elected officials tell the police to stand down while thugs run wild in the streets, we have to protect ourselves."

"Interesting," I paused to reflect before taking another angle. "You seem to be sincere but, no offense intended, I've seen it all. We've had some crazy callers in the past who were pretty convincing. Let me ask you something that only the Avenging Angel would know."

"Shoot."

"The recent incident in Chicago; you or a copycat?"

He laughed sardonically, "That's for me to know and you to find out."

I tried to shame him into slipping up, "What, have you got something against transparency? Who is this really, Joe Biden?"

"Very funny but insults will get you nowhere."

He was a tough nut so, I resorted to begging, "C'mon man, throw me a bone. Can't you give us a hint?"

"That would ruin the fun. *Clark Kent, Bruce Wayne, Peter Parker, Barry Allen* – all of us crime fighters have to protect our identities."

He stumped me on the last one, "Barry Allen?"

"C'mon 'Rambo' he's my favorite: The *Flash*."

"Oh yeah."

"Hey, I've got to go but maybe I'll check in again sometime. Keep fighting the good fight."

"Wait, can't you give us even a crumb regarding Chicago?"

"I'll only say this. I hope there will be other Avenging Angels who will stand up for freedom and liberty all across this country." The call ended abruptly.

"Wow, folks! Could it be? Did the real Avenging Angel just call into the 'Rambo' Show? I'd like to hear your opinion."

The first caller, Joey, wasn't impressed, "Naw, that guy was a fake."

"How do you know?"

"He didn't sound like a martial arts kind of guy." He hung up.

"Thank you, Joey. I'm glad you can tell a guy's self-defense skills by the sound of his voice." I tried to imitate Bruce Lee with a horrible Chinese accent that was intentionally flawed. "Next up is Donnie."

"Sounded like the real deal to me."

"How so? Do you think he had a martial arts voice?"

He guffawed in what sounded like a Texas drawl, "No, nothing like that. It was his logic."

"His logic? You must be a deep thinker, Donnie."

"Maybe so, maybe not. Common sense really. If he was faking, he would have made up a story about Chicago. The fact that he played it close to the vest sounded like what I'd do if I was trying to conceal my identity."

"Excellent point, Donnie!"

My listenership jumped through the roof when the word got out that I may have struck up an on-air relationship with the Avenging Angel. I tried to exploit the situation by replaying the interview several times and inviting AA to call back. However, there was no reply, at least not from the real Avenging Angel. Several imposters called to pick up the slack but I easily smoked them out. To my great disappointment, AA remained quiet.

In the meantime, Michael kept his 10:00 p. m. appointment the day he received the secret invitation from Officer Richard Morgan. Art Hill was a long, grassy slope leading down from the majestic St. Louis Art Museum to the reflecting pools well below. Normally, this would be anything but a private place to meet, especially during the daytime and on weekends. People loved to lounge, picnic, play, read, exercise and

walk all over the spacious grounds in this famous
section of Forest Park. Nighttime during the week
was a different matter. The high crime rate kept
people away and this had been exacerbated by the
violent riots that occurred at the top of the hill
around the massive statue of King Louis IX of
France, the City's sainted namesake.

Michael parked well away by the sheltered
dock where they stored the motorized rental boats
that putted around the manmade lake during
operating hours. Now deserted, no one else was
in sight. Michael couldn't see Art Hill due to the
large hedge of bushes that ran perpendicular to
the sidewalk. Once he'd cleared that obstacle he
turned and looked all the way up the long ascent
to see St. Louis, the stately crusader, atop his
trusty steed silhouetted against the lighted
backdrop beaming from the Art Museum. A
whisper caught him off guard, "Pssst, over here."

He whirled to find a shadowy figure coming
out of the nearby thicket. "You scared the heck
out of me!"

Richard hooted, "You, scared? The big, bad,
ninja crimefighter?"

Michael tried to laugh it off self-
deprecatingly, "Who me? Naw, I was just

kidding." He pretended to be wiping at his crotch, "Excuse me while I dry myself off."

"Okay funny man, enough of the comedy. Let's get down to business before we're interrupted."

"Are you serious? The only way we'll get interrupted around here is if someone tries to mug us. No one in their right mind would wander around here at night."

"Yep, that pretty much sums up the situation. At least one of us is not in our right mind." Michael dissed him with a sideways smile but let him continue. "Which brings me to the point of this meeting. Please tell me you didn't take a field trip to Chicago."

"Okay, if you want me to lie. I didn't go to Chicago."

"I knew it! You truly have lost your mind!"

Michael tried to justify what was clearly irrational. "Darnell-Wright took a powder and the anarchist-types in St. Louis were onto me. You wanted me to lay low, right?"

"Yeah but that didn't mean you should take your show on the road." Richard sighed hopelessly, "Why didn't you talk to me first?"

Michael stared in disbelief, "You made it sound like I'd be putting you in grave danger if I tried to contact you." Richard nodded reluctantly and the tension eased. "Besides, I felt terrible about putting you in harm's way with everything I'd done here in St. Louis. I didn't want you to be complicit with anything I did out of town."

Richard gave him a friendly pat on the shoulder, "I appreciate that Michael but you've got to understand. In for a penny, in for a pound. We're in this together from here on out whether I like it or not."

"So, you think what I did in Chicago was wrong?"

"Not wrong in the sense that I'm sure those bums had it coming, especially the gang banger who shot that baby girl." He placed both hands atop Michael's shoulders and bored into him with his eyes. "But this is only going to magnify our problem. This could even get the Feds involved if they think you're committing crimes across state lines."

Michael's lips curled up ever-so-slightly in a sly grin, "I don't have any control over what copycats might do."

"That's the only thing that's saving your butt right now." Richard exhaled long and loud, "Look. We need to somehow put Darnell-Wright on ice so you can be done with this."

Michael stunned the pragmatic cop, "It's bigger than that."

"What?"

"On a personal level, I can't stop until Sally has received justice. Beyond that, it's starting to take on a life of its own." Richard's jaw dropped as Michael tried to explain. "Getting Sally's due might satisfy me personally but what about all the other folks out there? There are hundreds, thousands of people just like Sally who are being bullied, beaten, robbed and worse. It's a question of basic freedom and safety. Somebody's got to stand up for the little guy."

"And that someone is you? Not the police? Not the authorities?"

Michael shot back, "So, we should put our faith and trust in local government while our buildings are burning and our heads are being bashed in?"

Richard seemed ready to explode when he took a long pause and several deep breaths.

"Okay, I hear you. But it will only get better if everyone, including you, respects the rule of law."

"I agree. Please tell that to Antifa and BLM." Richard crossed his arms in frustration but held his tongue. "Right now, we're at a crossroads. Until we've run that gauntlet, we the people are going to have to step up." He stretched out his palms appealing for sympathy, "I'm just doing my part."

Richard smiled and said as affectionately as possible, "All right you stubborn, dumb, jackass. I know your mind is set in concrete but at least take some precautions. Play it safe and smart."

"Trust me. I am." Michael went on to lay out his plan to visit other hot-spot cities while taking steps to leave no tracks back to him and St. Louis. "I'll feed the narrative that copycats are taking over elsewhere. For example, I might leave Eveready AAs in Portland and Rayovacs in Louisville." He chuckled, "The copper tops will be reserved strictly for St. Louis."

Richard shook his head in reluctant agreement, "Hopefully, things will be quiet around here."

"Yep, I'll lay low here at home. That is, unless Darnell-Wright turns up."

"Okay but please leave him to me for now. I'll let you know if I pick up the scent again."

"Deal!"

Michael didn't hear from Richard again until Richard heard about Michael being on my show. After listening to the podcast, Richard set up another secret meeting with AA; this time at the abandoned produce market in Soulard off Broadway. This once famous landmark had long been a thriving beehive of activity in South St. Louis near the Anheuser-Busch Brewery. Now, it was just a ghost town barely echoing the glorious traditions of the past. Within eyesight of the Arch and a stone's throw from the giant, red Budweiser sign atop A-B's Bevo packaging plant, this should have been a safe location. However, things had declined to where being there at night represented a tangible risk.

Even though it felt eerie to walk among the now-deserted stands along produce row, it brought back some fond memories to Michael of dickering with colorful shop keepers over the price of apples, oranges and bananas. A dark silhouette stepped out of the shadows. Although Michael's heart raced involuntarily, he was soon relieved to hear Richard's voice, "We meet again."

"Why do I feel like *James Bond*?"

Richard lamented, "I know. This seems silly but it is necessary."

"Yeah, I understand. So, what's on your mind?"

Even in a whisper, Richard's voice became quite animated, "I heard you on the 'Rambo' Show."

Michael declared proudly, "That was cool, wasn't it?"

"Are you kidding? You must have a screw loose!" Wyatt was dumbfounded and shrugged with his palms up. "Are you trying to draw attention? Really?"

Michael retorted soberly, "I'm trying to draw attention to a cause, not myself."

"That's just wonderful! Now, you're a rebel with a cause," he sniped. "Whether you realize it or not, you're not doing yourself any favors. There are powerful people in this town who would like nothing better than to lock you up and throw away the key. Your little publicity stunt has only increased their motivation."

Michael sounded sincerely offended, "I'm not concerned with the motivations of corrupt politicians and City officials. By going on that show, I wanted to offer some hope to the silent majority. Lord knows they need a little encouragement."

Richard took a moment to let the tension subside, "I know you're sincere and your intentions are good. I'm with you one-hundred percent on that count." He stopped to maintain his composure. "But it won't help anyone – you, me or the voiceless, nameless little guys out there – if they catch up with you."

Michael revealed his logic, "I know I'm taking a risk but I think it's worth it. Right now, they're shaping public opinion. The media and City officials have painted me as a crazed vigilante; a menace to society. This guy, Rooney, can help turn the tide."

Richard challenged, "Even if he could, how does winning a PR war help you?"

Michael revealed a practical side, "It would be more than a morale boost." Richard remained perplexed with his hands placed stubbornly on his hips. "Who is my greatest ally?" He didn't wait for an answer. "Yeah, that would be you. And you said most of your cop buddies were behind me even though there are obviously a few snakes in the woodpile."

"So, what does that have to do with you being on the radio?"

"You wouldn't be on my side if it wasn't for you knowing the truth." Richard nodded in agreement. "How can I expect support from anyone else as long as the media makes me out to be the villain?" Richard rubbed his chin thoughtfully. "If people understand the truth, they'll be more inclined to be in my corner. You never know. Someone out there might just save me some day if they think I'm a force for good."

"You've got a point there but still it's awfully risky."

"Does anything worthwhile come without some risk?" Richard shook his head. Michael laughed, "It's fair to say, I'm already risking quite a lot. Is it really pushing the envelope that much further to try to garner some favorable press?"

"When you put it that way, I guess not. We're already up to our necks in alligators. What's the harm of a few more?"

"Now, you're talking partner!"

"Partner? You're on your own on this one, pal."

"I wouldn't ask you to go on the radio with me. I'm not crazy."

"But?"

"But you could help me in convincing 'Rambo' Rooney to back us." Richard looked apoplectic but somehow held his tongue. "Let's meet with the guy in secret and fill him in on all the details."

"What? You want to give him enough rope to hang us?"

"No. I don't think he'd turn on us. Have you listened to him? He's a true patriot – a real believer."

Chapter 13:

AA called the show one morning but didn't ask to come on the air. During a commercial break, my producer said, "That guy is back on the line."

"Who, the Avenging Angel; the real guy?"

"Yep, it sounds like him."

"Then put him through right after the break."

"He says he doesn't want to come on the air. Says he wants to talk to you privately."

I didn't have to think for long, "Okay, give him my private cell number and ask him to call me as soon as we're off the air."

After closing the show, I sweated bullets for ten minutes thinking that he'd changed his mind. Then the phone rang and I tried not to sound overly excited, "This is Dylan."

"Sorry, I must have called the wrong number. I was looking for 'Rambo' Rooney," he snickered.

"Very funny. Thanks for calling, AA."

"You recognized my voice?"

"Maybe. Let's just say it was a good guess. Anyway, to what do I owe the pleasure?" I didn't give him a chance to answer before I peppered him, "We've missed you. My listeners have been clamoring to hear from you again."

"Perhaps that can be arranged."

I didn't want to appear too eager but couldn't help it. This guy was ratings gold. "How about tomorrow morning? Or better yet, how about a regular slot on the show?"

"Whoa, whoa, slow down. We need to clear up a few things first."

I tried to hide my disappointment, "Okay, you're the boss."

"I'd like to give you exclusive access." My heart almost popped out of my chest. "But not necessarily on the air."

The bottom dropped out and I couldn't help but sound deflated, "Exclusive access to what then?"

"To my story."

"But you won't come on the air? You do realize that I'm in the radio business, right?"

AA explained, "I'll tell you everything your audience needs to know. You can relay it on the air."

"Why can't you share it with them directly?"

"It's too risky. Even talking with you privately would put me in great jeopardy but I'm trusting that you would protect my identity."

AA went on to explain that he'd share details that no one else could know and allow me to chronicle them in any fashion at my discretion. Finally, I had to get down to the brass tacks, "So, what's in it for you?"

"Simple. I want the people out there to know the truth. Right now, the media has painted me in a horrible light. You can correct that."

I challenged, "But why? Why even take the chance?"

"Because our country is in real trouble. Somebody's got to step up and fight for the truth. You have your way and I have mine. I figure we can do more for our country by combining forces."

"Okay, I'll buy that. Obviously, you believe in the cause of freedom, liberty and justice or you wouldn't be going out on such a limb. But you're asking me to take you at your word. How can I know that your side of the story is accurate if I can't challenge you on the air and allow callers to question you?"

AA dropped a bombshell, "I think I can help you there too." I listened with baited breath. "There's someone in law enforcement who may be willing to corroborate my story."

I couldn't believe my ears, "A cop?"

"Don't get ahead of yourself. First, my friend would need every assurance that you'd protect his identity too."

"Okay, how do I convince your friend?"

"We'd like to meet with you, privately. You'd have to agree to be blindfolded."

This sounded really weird but I didn't want to look a gift horse in the mouth so I blurted, "Done."

Three days later, I found myself in an awkward situation. Following AA's precisely detailed instructions, I stood on my front porch with my back to the street. The lights on the porch and in the front rooms were off so, I was wrapped in darkness. Although the chances were slim on a weeknight, I guessed the blackout was meant to ensure that I wouldn't draw the attention of any night-owl neighbors. At 11:00 p. m., a car pulled up and I forced myself to keep looking straight ahead at the door just inches in front of my nose. The car hesitated for a moment then rolled on by slowly. *Was it a nosy neighbor scoping me out?* This question was answered when they came back around the block again and stopped.

I heard the door open and footsteps treaded toward me. At first, I was shocked when I didn't recognize the voice, "Don't move." I tensed up. "Take it easy, I'm going to slip this hood over your head." It was a linen sack that allowed me to breathe through the hood but still it made me feel terribly claustrophobic. He took me by the elbow and carefully led me away from the porch. I heard another car door open and the stranger protected my head as I bent over to get in.

My heart was racing until I heard AA's voice, "I'm sorry for all the cloak and dagger stuff but you understand." I nodded. "I'd like you to meet my friend. You can call him Harry." He clasped my hand firmly and shook it.

"Nice to meet you, Harry."

"Likewise."

We drove around for about fifteen or twenty minutes before the car came to a rest. From the silence, I gathered that we were in a deserted area; maybe a parking lot or down an old, blacktop road out in the sticks. Since I lived in St. Charles it didn't take long to get out in the wide-open spaces. The only sound I could make out was intermittent but fairly constant road noise faintly off in the distance. Apparently, we were someplace close to an interstate where some level of traffic continued at all hours. Then, not too far away, I heard railroad cars passing by as if from above. My guess was that we were down by the old rail bridge that crossed over the Missouri River. If that was the case, they'd chosen well because no one would bother us there.

For a good twenty minutes they took turns grilling me. Harry sounded like a cop who'd interrogated many a criminal in his day. As an experienced interviewer myself, I could appreciate their methodology. They did everything possible to rattle me such as shifting the pace from slow to rapid fire and changing the tone from friendly to accusatory. I did my best to be myself and answer questions in an honest, straightforward and consistent manner. They even got philosophical to, I guessed, gauge my bona fides as a died-in-the-wool, patriotic conservative.

Apparently, I passed muster because AA asked point blank, "Do you want to know our identities?"

"It would help," I wanted to slap myself for sounding a little shaky.

"Do you give us your solemn word that you'll never reveal our true identities without our permission?"

I tried not to hesitate but paused slightly because I realized this was a significant commitment, perhaps with legal implications despite freedom of the press. "Yes, you have my word."

The one called Harry broke in sternly, "Do you understand that once you've learned our identities and we've shared the Avenging Angel's story in full detail," now he sounded like a lawyer, "and since you've committed to concealing our identities, you could be held legally liable as an accessory?"

This got my hackles up to where I couldn't help being snarky, "What's next officer? Are you going to read me my Miranda rights?"

This earned me a swift redress, "Listen smart guy, we don't need this. I'd be more than happy to let you out right here to walk home."

AA jumped in to avoid a breakdown, "I'm sorry Rooney but we're putting everything on the line here. If you want to collaborate with us, we need your full and unqualified commitment." He left no doubt about his intentions for me, "In for a penny, in for a pound."

At the point of no return, I gave myself plenty of time to think it through and they waited patiently. *Was I willing to stick my neck out? They certainly were. But was the cause worth it?* I considered the state of our country, a country on the brink of anarchy and socialism. It was no exaggeration to believe that our constitutional republic was hanging by a thread so, I threw caution to the wind. I proudly declared, "What the hell. All for one and one for all!"

I felt like I was a character in one of those Mafia movies where a newly made man was taking the vow of omerta or silence. A hand grabbed the top of my hood and slowly lifted it off of my head. "Welcome to the crew. I'm Officer Richard Morgan of the St. Louis Police."

The other fellow behind the wheel chimed in, "I'm Michael Wyatt." I felt woozy. It seemed like the gravity of seeing them face-to-face made the blood rush to my head. Wyatt must have noticed because he tried to lighten the mood with a goofy grin as he added, "My enemies call me the Avenging Angel."

I tried to respond in kind by chiding Officer Morgan, "I guess your enemies call you *Dirty Harry*?"

They both busted out with uproarious laughter that seemed out of place. "What, what did I say?"

After settling down and wiping his eyes, Richard explained, "Sorry man. It's an inside joke."

"Please, fill me in."

"Actually, my nickname IS *Dirty Harry*, the black version. I'm old-school; not a participation trophy kind of guy. My approach to crime fighting is that sometimes you've just got to kick ass and take names."

Now it was my turn to bust out laughing as I offered Morgan a hearty high-five. Once things settled down, we stared at each other with what-now looks. I decided to strike while the iron was hot, "Let's get down to business."

AA replied, "It's late fellas. Some of us have to get up early for work in the morning."

I offered, "Want to get together at my house tomorrow night?"

Richard brought me up to speed, "We can't be seen together. No emails, no texts and no phone calls either – unless you use a burner phone."

"Isn't that taking things kind of far?"

Richard's glare had a sobering effect on me, "There are some powerful people trying to identify the Avenging Angel. They want to crush him, everything he stands for and anyone who might be helping him."

"Oh," I gulped.

"They'd bury you, me and him without blinking. For your own protection, not just ours, we can't be linked together." I stared blankly. "This place is as out-of-the-way as it gets. Let's meet here Thursday night at the same time." Things were pretty quiet on the ride home to drop me off.

Richard's diagnosis of the situation hit me hard as I realized I may have bitten off more than I could chew. *Would I be able to hide behind my First Amendment rights if my broadcasting earned the attention of the police?* With my mind spinning and stomach churning, I couldn't sleep a wink so, I turned on the news and poured three fingers of straight bourbon into a tumbler. As I watched a recap of the day's insane politicking, rampant lying, brazen corruption and mindless rioting and violence, it gave me new resolve. Sure, I'd taken a huge and perhaps needless risk but it was worth it. As the booze took effect and I hit the sack, my final thought was, *desperate times call for desperate measures.*

I felt some butterflies as Thursday night approached. It reminded me of my days as a high school football player preparing for a big game. After crossing over the bridge on I-70, I circled back toward the river via the Earth City Expressway and St. Charles Rock Road. After turning left, I followed it to where the Rock Road ended at an old bottom road that was rarely used. There was a riverside sand-dredging operation on the left and junk yard on the right. Then I passed the entrance to a paintball park further down on the left. Of course, nothing was open at that time of night. Thereafter, the old, unmaintained road continued for a half-mile or so.

It narrowed to one lane because the vegetation was encroaching from both sides. In the eerie darkness it seemed as though witches and goblins were stretching out their spindly arms to impede my progress. A yellow, metal sign marked the dead end. Despite reading, "No Dumping," it was apparent many scofflaws had ignored the warning. Off to the side were several large piles of old, broken-down furniture, discarded tires, abandoned appliances and such. It gave me the willies being in such a dark desolate place that seemed like a perfect hideout for an ax-murderer or chainsaw-wielding maniac. Consequently, I turned my SUV around before exiting; just in case I needed to get out of there fast.

The view above reminded me of an old horror movie. The ancient but sturdy-looking wooden trestles were stacked about fifty feet high. With my head cocked back, I could see the outline of the rails stretching across the top, silhouetted against a full moon encircled by ominous clouds. As if on cue, the spooky hooting of a nearby owl sent a jolt up my spine. Otherwise, it was starkly quiet except for the distant buzz of traffic on the interstate. The fall chill had stilled the crickets and frogs. The highway lent an odd, soothing peacefulness that settled my nerves with its monotonous, droning melody.

A pair of distant headlights yanked my psyche back onto high alert. I peered anxiously until I recognized Michael Wyatt's car. I had to cover my eyes from the high beams until they dimmed when he turned off the ignition. My pupils were still adjusting when Morgan hopped out of the passenger side and quipped, "Ready for a fast getaway, eh?"

"You've got to admit it's kind of creepy out here."

He let me off the hook, "That's why we chose this spot. No one in their right mind would come out here alone – unless they wanted to dump their trash or a dead body," he teased.

AA opened his trunk and pulled out some folding chairs, "Might as well make ourselves comfortable." He set them up in a little circle. Before we could plop down, he reached into a cooler and handed each of us a cold Budweiser. "This could take a while. We might as well enjoy ourselves." He smiled broadly, "This Bud's for you, old pal!"

"Old pal?"

"Yeah, I remember you from school."

"Oh, did you go to Mizzou too?"

"No, I'm talking high school. You were a legend at Pattonville."

"Did you graduate from there too?"

"Yep, I'm a fellow Pirate."

"Did you play football?"

"Yes, but I was nothing like you. Even though you preceded me by a decade, you were still iconic."

I tried to downplay it since those glory days were long gone, "I did all right."

"All right? That was the first time any Pirate football team made it to the state finals. And you were not only the best player but the team captain!"

Richard had had enough of our walk down memory lane and AA's fawning devotion. He remarked dismissively, "Okay, okay – go team, go Pirates. I doubt you're interested in my basketball prowess, since I lived in the hood."

AA proved him wrong by enthusiastically inquiring, "Where'd you go?"

"Vashon. Didn't have the benefit of no white privilege there," he teased.

AA exclaimed, "Wow, the Wolverines were tough! How many state championships did you guys win in basketball?"

"Lost count preppie. Anyway, can we move on?"

I couldn't resist gigging Richard a bit, "How about your football team?"

"Yeah, yeah – we sucked. Couldn't hold a candle to the mighty Pirates." As he paused to think, he smiled as though he might bust out laughing, "I've got a nickname for you two: *The Captain and Tennille.*"

I was impressed at Richard's recall. It had been a long time since the 1970s icons, "Captain" Daryl Dragon and Toni Tennille had topped the charts. "I'm surprised that a kid from the hood would still remember a couple of white pop stars from ancient history."

The black *Dirty Harry* quipped, "I've always been a leader in diversity."

AA feigned offense at being feminized, "How dare you question my masculinity like that!"

Richard conceded, sort of, "Okay, I'll change the nickname. You can stay AA but 'Rambo' here will henceforth have a secret code name in our private, little group: Captain Bucco."

I played along, "I like that! Yeah, Captain Bucco – the king of the Pirates." The funny thing was, it stuck.

It was late so Richard prodded us, "All right, enough funny business."

I pulled out an old Dictaphone, "Do you mind if I record our conversation?"

Richard jumped in, "Do you promise not to play it back on the air?"

"Duly noted, Officer," I saluted. "This is just to save me from taking notes. I promise I'll never play this for anyone else."

Richard quizzed me, "Why not just use your phone?"

"With this thing, I can burn the tape and it's gone. Once you record something on your phone, it's somewhere in the Cloud forever."

"Good thinking."

AA went back to the beginning and shared everything in great detail; a blow-by-blow account. Richard broke in at intervals to corroborate everything he could. From time-to-time, I asked clarifying questions but not too often because their testimony was so fascinating and compelling, I didn't want to interrupt. Some of my inquiries were just nudges to get them both to share what they were feeling at the time. This would help add a human element to their story. The whole process took several hours but I never got tired. Their accounts kept me on the edge of my seat.

Once they were finished, I offered this general observation, "You were right. Even though we were aligned philosophically, I couldn't have imagined the full and true motivation behind your actions without hearing your direct testimony. I not only believe you but now I can believe IN you."

AA replied, "That means a lot to me. I know in my own heart that I'm not a villain. At my core, I'm not an outlaw. I respect the rule of law and I delight in God's commands."

"That's right, Michael, you're the good guy. You're a real-life, crime-fighting crusader."

Richard chided, "Don't give him a big head," but offered AA a congratulatory fist bump to show he agreed with me.

"One thing amazes me though."

AA asked, "What's that?"

"How do you keep it separate?"

"Keep what separate?"

"Your personal stake in the matter versus fighting for the greater good?"

"I don't know if I can keep them separate," I stared inquisitively. "This started as nothing more than a highly personalized battle to achieve justice for Sally." He halted and looked skyward before continuing. "Somewhere along the way, I realized we're all in this together. Sally and I weren't just the victims of four local thugs. Our whole country has been victimized. Freedom is worth fighting for; always has been and, hopefully, always will be." He looked at me apologetically. "I couldn't stand on the sidelines and watch while the liberty that so many had fought and died for was stolen."

It was late and I really needed to catch a couple hours of sleep before taking to the air so, I economized my feelings with these few words. "Thank you so much, Michael. I'll try to do my best to support what you're doing. And thank you too, Officer Morgan."

"That's Richard to you, me Bucco."

Chapter 14:

They'd given me everything I needed so, I was off and running. Despite the lack of sleep, my excitement level was through the roof as I took to the air. I had more than enough material to fill up days, no, weeks of airtime. The audience's response was even better than expected. Our ratings took off like an F-18 Hornet scrambling under red alert. The only problem was that, with so much information to dispense, I couldn't accept as many callers. Nevertheless, the lines were so jammed that I cut into my own dialogue to take a few questions. "Welcome to the show, Kevin. What's on your mind?"

"I'm a first-time caller."

"Great! Thanks for joining in."

"Hey, uh, 'Rambo,' let me ask. Let me ask you a question, uh, Mr. 'Rambo.'"

It sounded like the guy was on speed while suffering from Tourette's Syndrome. I cleared my throat, "Kev," but couldn't get more than one syllable out before he talked over me.

His words exploded in rapid-fire fashion like a machine gun was stuck in his throat. "Yeah, been listening to you talk about that AA guy. You know, the Avenging Angel. Are you telling me that you actually talked to this guy? Did he phone you? Did you meet face-to-face? What does he look like? I mean, big guy, little guy? White dude? Did he demonstrate any of that jujitsu stuff, um MMA, um karate, whatever? Why's he doing this stuff? Is he coming on the air again? What about the uh, the uh, copycat? How do you, um you 'Rambo' know him? What's his real name? I mean, people want to know this stuff, Mr. 'Rambo.'" You know?"

"Whoa, Kevin, hold on there! Let me catch up. Gee whiz, folks. I think Kevin has just established a new land-speed record for the most questions asked by a caller within a twenty-second period." I had to laugh at the absurdity of the caller's staccato assault. "I'll never be able to remember everything you just asked me and, heaven knows, I'm not going to ask you to repeat the questions. But let me see if I can get at the gist of your curiosity."

"Okay, uh okay, uh, thank you, Mr. 'Rambo' sir. I'll hang up and, uh, uh, listen."

"For all of you listeners out there, Kevin actually touched on an important point. If I understood that amazing barrage of questions, he basically wants to know whether my account is credible." My producer cut in with a ding, ding, ding gameshow-winner sound effect. "Here's what I can and cannot tell you. Everything I've chronicled before you came from a primary source. In legal terms, it would be called first-person testimony. Additionally, in many cases it has been corroborated by an independent source."

I paused to let that sink in before explaining further. "That means, you can take it to the bank. It's not second or third-hand accounts. Straight from the horse's mouth folks and independently verified by yours truly."

The phone lines blew up so, I took another caller. "How can we believe you when we haven't heard from your sources directly?"

"Have I ever lied to you in all my years of broadcasting? Don't you listen to my show because I'm the only one in this town who will give it to you straight?"

"I agree 'Rambo' but why can't you shed more light on your sources?"

"Ethics. Journalistic integrity requires that I protect my sources and the Constitution protects me in doing so. Think about it this way. Would you want me to name my sources and throw them to the wolves just to satisfy your curiosity? The

Avenging Angel is doing this to fight corruption. AA is taking great risks on your behalf as well as mine in order to stand up for liberty, freedom and justice. We've got to have his back."

"Yeah, when you put it that way, you're right. Thanks, 'Rambo' and keep up the good fight."

While my local show was dominated by my chronicles of the Avenging Angel, the national media turned most of its focus to the election, now only weeks away. They turned a blind eye to a horrendous spectacle out of Louisville where a black Trump supporter organized a peaceful demonstration in favor of law enforcement. For his trouble, a large Antifa mob attacked the much smaller group and bashed out the organizer's front teeth.

It would have been swept completely under the rug if not for one specific repercussion. Someone tracked down the bat-wielding malefactor and beat him to a pulp. The mainstream media couldn't bury the story because, when the police found the bloodied Antifa thug, he was adorned with a string-necklace from which hung a winged AA Energizer.

The thug's generic description didn't help much. His white attacker was tall but he couldn't say much about his face or build since he was dressed in a loose-fitting, black hoodie with a matching mask. When asked about karate skills, the thug admitted, "Naw, none of that stuff. Dude just whupped me old-style with his fists." The only distinguishing piece of evidence the media could latch onto was the calling card. Noting how AA had never fashioned a necklace before and preferred copper top batteries, the press ran with the copycat narrative.

I received a call from Michael on a burner phone. "You had me worried the other day."

"How's that?"

"When that crazy, motor-mouth guy called into the show, I thought you might give me up."

"Michael, you know me better than that."

He laughed, "Just kidding. But I can guarantee you that Richard's butt was puckered up," he laughed even harder. In his jovial mood, I couldn't tell if he was still pulling my leg when he asked, "Hey, did you hear about that copycat guy in Louisville?"

"Yeah." I waited for more but AA left me hanging so, I bit. "Was that you?"

"Hey, don't you read the papers? They're sure it was a copycat."

"C'mon, Michael, level with me. It was you, wasn't it?"

"I may have been in Louisville by coincidence." This time I applied the pregnant pause. "They have some great barbeque down there." Still, I kept my mouth shut. "What would you say if I told you it was me?"

"Honestly, I'd say that puke deserved it. Moreover, I'd give you a high-five the next time I saw you." I stopped to mull over the details again. "A couple of things didn't add up."

"What's that?"

"The necklace and no karate."

He roared with laughter, "Pretty good, huh?" He sounded proud of himself without being boastful. "I didn't think that the switch to Eveready alone was enough to throw them off. As for the ban on karate, frankly, I didn't need it. I caught the guy alone, without his Antifa pals, and was able to take him out with some good, old-fashioned pugilism."

"Well, congratulations because it seemed to work. They swallowed the copycat thing whole."

"I wish Richard would have too."

"Oh?"

"He's pissed. Read me the riot act. He's under the false impression that this will all be over once he nabs Darcy Darnell-Wright."

"And that's not the case?"

"First of all, that guy could be dead or hiding out in Mexico for all we know."

"And secondly?"

"This is bigger than Sally, me and the 'King.'"

I tried to be the voice of reason. "I know you're doing this for the right reasons and you're looking out for the beleaguered silent majority. But you've got to think of your future too. This can't go on forever. It won't end well."

"Maybe so but there's a hell of a lot more at stake here than my future." He paused before continuing with resolve beyond sternness. "I don't have a future without Sally."

"You've got to trust God, Michael. Leave it in his hands."

"I know. I just wish I had something to occupy my mind. I'm going crazy." I had no words of wisdom to offer. "If only I could get a lead on Darnell-Wright, I'd have purpose. I'd have a goal."

Soon thereafter, his prayers were answered in a most unexpected way. Feeling forlorn, Michael went to pay a visit to Sally even though his heart wasn't in it. After barely greeting the staff, he shuffled into Sally's room with slumped shoulders and the empty expression of someone drowning in depression. The all-too-familiar, morbid surroundings did nothing to lift him from his pity pit. That is, until he discerned something slightly out of place. Someone had left an unopened card on the stand next to Sally's bed. As he moved closer to retrieve it, he felt one of those heart-stopping jolts sometimes delivered at the end of horror movies like *Carrie* or *Friday the 13th*.

The envelope was addressed in hand-written, block letters, "To: sAAlly." With his fingers fumbling frantically, Michael tore open the envelope and pulled out the card. Something fell out when he opened the card. When he rushed to bend down and pick up the object, he bumped his head on the stand. This evoked a natural anger reflex that hit ten on the Richter Scale when

Michael recognized the contents as a foil square containing a condom. He scrambled to read the note inside the card, "AA, have you missed me? Please let Sally know we haven't forgotten about her." It was unsigned but the author had drawn a crude phallic symbol adorned with a crown to leave no doubt.

Michael's Papa Bear-instinct kicked in with a vengeance. His first move was to head out to the nurse's station and ask who had delivered the note. When no one seemed to have a clue, he thought about getting the guards involved to review security footage from the video cameras. Thankfully, he caught himself by realizing that they'd want to inspect the note carefully. He'd be exposed once they understood the AA reference. Consequently, he carefully tailored his inquiry saying that the note was from a long-lost friend with whom he wanted to reconnect. With the note tucked away firmly, he continued his altruistic line of questioning.

Finally, one of the nurses just back from her rounds explained, "I put the note in Sally's room."

"Where did you get it? Did someone drop it off at the nurse's station or the front desk in the lobby?" Michael desperately wanted to establish the possible existence of video evidence.

"No, it was kind of strange. When I went out on my lunch break, this fellow down at *Five Guys* noticed my uniform and asked if I knew your wife. When I said yes, he asked if I could drop off a get-well card. I told him that visiting hours were open and he was welcome to deliver it personally. He claimed he was a friend of the family but, unfortunately, was in a rush to leave for the airport." She looked apologetic, "What could I do? He handed it to me and rushed out the door."

Michael spoke in an easy tone as if totally unconcerned, "Oh, it's no problem. By the way, was he a tall, black fellow with a scar on his cheek?"

"Yes, as a matter of fact, he was."

Michael did his best to conceal the terror he felt, "Yeah, that's our dear friend, Darcy."

"Is everything okay?"

"Oh, I'm just disappointed. I've been wanting to get back in touch with him for a long time." The nurse smiled empathetically. "In any case, it's so good to hear from him. Thank you," he lied.

This prompted another clandestine meeting of the three amigos. Under the moonlit shadow of the railroad trestles, Michael dramatically declared, "This is a total game-changer." Before I could ask why, he turned to me with a flinty look in his eyes. "This is NOT for public consumption. I'm keeping you in the loop since we're all in this together but do NOT air any of this on your show."

"Easy, Michael. Whatever you say. Mum's the word," I pretended to zip my mouth shut.

He explained what had happened and showed us the note and condom. "Needless to say, I won't be going on any road trips until this threat has been removed."

Richard tried to calm him down, "This is the first tactical error Darnell-Wright has made." He massaged his chin thoughtfully. "Something serious must have brought him out of hiding."

I asked, "How so?"

"This dude is clever as you can tell by the way he avoided video surveillance." I nodded. "He wouldn't take the risk without a good reason." He turned to Michael, "This guy's too smart and cautious to taunt you just for the sake of rattling your cage. No, he's trying to lure you out."

"Are you sure?" I posed.

"Yep, there's no other reasonable explanation. He knew for certain that, by threatening Sally and in such a vulgar way, he'd bait you, Michael. He wants to take out AA."

My reporter's instincts kicked in, "But why now?"

"I don't know but he must be desperate. My guess is that he's getting hit in the pocket book. AA put a big dent in his revenue stream when he forced him into hiding. That, or perhaps someone is trying to take up the slack in his absence by encroaching on his turf."

"That makes sense." Another thought occurred, "If he knows Michael's identity, why doesn't he just turn him into the police?"

"He can't take the chance of inadvertently associating himself with Michael in a way that could reopen a can of worms. That might mess up the way the City has conveniently covered up his crimes against Sally. No, he wants to get rid of AA quietly and permanently and eliminate the threat altogether."

I exclaimed as this sunk in, "This is a real mess. Darnell-Wright can't go to the cops but neither can Michael unless he's willing to own up to being AA."

Richard concluded, "Yeah, unfortunately, we've got to continue to deal with this on the sly. The important thing is that he wants Michael enraged to the point of doing something foolish." He turned to Michael, this time with his most authoritative cop glare. "That's why you need to stay put. We're not going to take the bait. This is where I step in. He won't be expecting that. Am I right?"

Michael responded compliantly, "Of course, you're right." Richard's eyes bored in on him. "Really, we've already been down this road." Richard didn't let up. "I won't make that mistake again."

He eased up and tried to reassure Michael, "Don't worry. Now that he's out and about again, I'll get him."

Even though I was aware of Michael's past indiscretions, I felt comfortable that he meant it when he promised not to interfere with Richard's police work. Thus, I turned back to my immediate concern. "In the meantime, what can I say on the air?"

Richard spoke for both of them, "Go back to doing what you were doing. Get the word out about everything that's transpired up to this point."

"But I can't mention anything about AA's personal redress?"

"Listen Bucco, you don't need to impress us with your vocabulary. If you mean, can you talk about what drove AA to get involved in the first place, the answer is yes." This gave me a lift before he clamped down. "But watch how you say it! No names and no details."

"No details?"

"Nothing specific enough that it could lead back to Michael." My face must have reflected my confusion. "Look, you can talk about AA experiencing a personal tragedy at the hands of some thugs involved in the riots. You can mention how a loved one was brutally beaten to the point of death. But, for example, don't say it was his wife. Don't say where it occurred. Not a peep that could point to DD-W or any member of his crew. Think before you speak and when in doubt, don't bring it out."

I heaved a sigh of relief, "Okay, I've got it. I can share enough details in general to serve the purpose. That is, to show that Michael isn't a vigilante driven by mindless rage. He's paid a personal price and now wants to make sure others don't suffer the same fate at the hands of the anarchists and opportunists." He gave me a thumbs up. "Will you guys keep me up to speed in the meantime?"

Richard assured me, "We'll call you when need be." He glanced back toward Michael and re-emphasized, "Burner phones only."

At that point, I was basically riding solo. I had no way of knowing how Morgan's pursuit of Darnell-Wright was going. As for Michael, I assumed he was towing the line and laying low. My frustration rose with each passing day. I wished I had a way of touching base but was at their mercy. It was a one-way street of information flow.

Nevertheless, I had plenty to keep me busy. Chronicling AA's story and keeping up with the looming election was more than enough to fill up my air time and then some. I didn't know about the other two sides of our triangle but, as for me, I succeeded in making AA's case. At least, that's how it seemed based on the reaction from our listeners. Even some of my detractors elsewhere in the media appeared to take note. They didn't abandon their narrative but at least acknowledged there was another side to the story, however implausible they tried to shade it.

Chapter 15:

Being completely in the dark at the time, I didn't know that Richard's prediction came to fruition almost immediately. Darnell-Wright wasn't hard to pin down once he took full control of his operation again. He was easy pickings for Officer Morgan, or so he thought. Unfortunately, Richard made the mistake of underestimating the crafty crook. As the eager cop prepared to go in for the kill, he never suspected that a trap had been laid.

"King" Darcy hadn't forgotten how "Onion" Brown had been done in by Morgan. He knew AA was being aided by his inside-man on the force. Borrowing from that script, Darnell-Wright staged a conspicuous, nightly fling that placed him regularly at the apartment of a femme fatale who was in on the ruse. Richard caught on right away and staked out the location just waiting for the right moment when the couple was alone and probable cause existed.

On night three, it all came together perfectly, too perfectly. The amorous couple appeared to have no inhibitions since the lights in the apartment were on and the thin shade didn't leave much to the imagination. Something rankled the young woman and romance turned to rage. Yelling and screaming led to DD-W's silhouette launching the young woman's shadow across the room. Richard bolted from his police cruiser and dashed up the stairs. Luckily, he thought, the door wasn't even locked so, he burst in, "Don't move!" he commanded forcefully with his gun drawn.

Almost immediately, he knew something was wrong. The young woman, naked to the world, didn't blush or bat an eye. She laughed knowingly as she casually reached for her nightgown. Also naked as a J-bird, the "King" casually scratched his privates while grinning evilly at Morgan who ordered, "Put your hands up! Both of you!"

He didn't hear the closest door behind him over the sound of his own voice. Then a sickening chill ran down his spine and parked in his gut as he heard someone from behind say, "Drop it, pig!"

When he turned his head, he saw two thugs with guns trained on him. Richard slowly set his gun down on the floor while being careful not to make any sudden movements. Darnell-Wright was already getting dressed. His supposed girlfriend sat down, still smiling, and casually lit a cigarette. Richard, the consummate professional, transitioned seamlessly into negotiation mode. If nothing else, he wanted to at least buy some time with the hope that another cruiser might happen by. "My precinct knows I'm investigating you. If I don't report back in, this is the first place they'll come looking." It was a lie. He'd purposefully hid his pursuit of Darnell-Wright to protect AA but they didn't know that. "In my world, cop-killers are the worst. They'll hunt you down and next stop, death row."

This didn't wipe the smirk off of Darnell-Wright's face. "Don't worry, boss man. We're not going to kill you – not here at least," he snorted. He picked up a gun and tucked it into his waistband. "Let's see if we can find someplace better. Maybe we'll stumble on some domestic violence where you might accidentally take a bullet. Or, better yet, let's find a drug deal going down where you can go out in a blaze of glory."

The three thugs arrogantly marched Richard down the steps. They didn't seem at all worried about interference from the neighbors. Richard figured they all knew better than to cross the gang leader. Morgan's mind raced as he calculated the risk of making a break. They didn't want to leave any clues for the cops but might shoot him anyway figuring they could dispose of the body elsewhere. *Could he zig-zag his way to freedom without getting hit?* The chances were slim with three of them but he knew one thing for sure. If he got into their car, it would be curtains.

Darnell-Wright had been savvy using "Onion's" demise to spring the trap but, in his smugness, overlooked one key element from the prior incident. He assumed that, since he was now the one being hunted, AA would remain in hiding and let his cop buddy handle the dirty work alone. Morgan was sweating bullets as they exited the doorway at the bottom of the stairs and stepped out onto the apartment building's stoop. It was now or never if he wanted to chance making a break.

For the first time, Richard was happy, no ecstatic, about Michael breaking his vow to keep his nose out of his police work. AA stepped from behind a parked car next to the curb, settled into a shooting crouch and barked, "Drop your guns!"

Everyone froze for just a moment and Richard immediately seized the opportunity to turn to Darnell-Wright who was behind him. "I'll take that," he said as he grabbed for his gun. It fell and clattered a few feet away. Then all hell broke loose as one of the thugs in front of Richard shouted a stream of profanities as he opened fire on AA. Michael didn't budge but firmly squeezed off a round that hit the shooter dead center.

The other thug launched a hail of bullets at Michael who dove behind the parked car. Richard shoved him from behind, jumped off the side of the staircase and tumbled to the ground. By the time Morgan was able to scramble to his feet and start running for cover, the thug had regained his footing and took aim. The shot hit Richard square in the butt and he collapsed in a heap, wincing in pain. The fallen officer watched helplessly in horror as the shooter rushed forward and stood over him ready to deliver the kill shot. He screamed, "Die pig!" as a shot rang out.

Richard had closed his eyes, expecting death to pierce his skull. But the only thing he felt was the weight of the dead thug's body crumpling on top of him. When he opened his eyes, Michael stood a few yards away, still in his shooting stance. He had recovered just in time to save the life of his friend. Although it was totally out of place, somehow it seemed like the only way to cut through the tragedy was with humor as Michael deadpanned, "Man, I'm really sorry I broke my promise."

Richard replied, "I've never been so happy about somebody backsliding on me," he erupted in laughter before abruptly groaning in agony.

Michael rushed to his aid, "Are you okay?"

Richard grunted through clenched teeth, "Pain in the ass." Michael must have assumed his pal had changed his mind about forgiving him because mournful regret washed over his face. The fallen officer grimaced as he turned on his side and grabbed his butt. "No, not you, dummy. I got shot right in the ass." Michael chortled at his friend's predicament. "You'll excuse me if I don't join in – it only hurts when I laugh." Michael crowed so loud that Richard couldn't contain his funny bone, that is, until his snickers were pinched off by the stinging jolts that shot through his tail end.

Michael tried to use his burner phone to dial 911 but was stopped by Richard, "What about Darnell-Wright?"

"He was hiding in the stairwell out of the line of fire. When I hit the deck, he took off like a banshee down the street in the opposite direction." Richard groaned louder than before. "I've gotta call 911. We need an ambulance."

Richard corrected Michael, "That wasn't because of the pain in my butt. We're screwed now."

"What?"

"Darnell-Wright. This might push him over the edge to squeal on us to save his own skin. If he panics, we're dead." Michael went pale at the prospect of being outed. "Snap out of it, man. I'm not giving up yet," Richard commanded.

"But."

"But nothing. Right now, the only butt I'm worried about is this one with the extra hole in it." Richard stretched out both hands toward Michael. "Help me up. I need to get back in my cruiser."

"You can't drive!"

"I know that. I need to call this in on my radio."

"Oh."

"And you need to get out of here pronto."

"Are you sure you'll be okay?"

"I'll be fine." Michael turned to leave but Richard stopped him. "Remember. You weren't here."

"But what about Darnell-Wright."

"It will be my word against his."

Richard's judgment proved accurate. Darnell-Wright took his case to the police but not in desperation. Rather than putting his own freedom in jeopardy, he went through informal channels. DD-W met secretly with a dirty cop who was on the thug's payroll. He pretended not to know AA's true identity but tied Officer Richard Morgan to the vigilante and his crimes. That way, he figured, he wouldn't have to answer for Sally but would take Richard out of commission. With him sidelined and Michael Wyatt left with no one to protect his flank, he felt confident he could take care of the thorn in his side, AA, for good.

Richard did his best to counter the charges as they filtered through the system. He said he was being framed by the guy in charge of the drug deal he'd stumbled onto. Morgan's story fit the facts of the matter. The two dead guys were, in fact, involved in drug dealing according to their records. When asked about the kingpin, Richard credibly stated that the man had escaped during the gun battle. When asked for a description of the escaped dealer, he lied and said he hadn't gotten a descent look at him in all the confusion. When challenged, he had the perfect comeback, "I was on the ground with a slug in my ass!"

He was lucky he was black and had been shot because the City didn't bother with autopsies or ballistics tests that would have revealed that the bullets didn't come from Morgan's gun. If he'd been white or the dead perps weren't armed, all hell would have broken loose. As things were, there probably still would have been riots if Richard hadn't been laid up in the hospital with a gunshot wound. That's how crazy things had become in St. Louis and cities all across America. But again, by the luck of the draw, there was relative calm because the mob's masters didn't want anything politically harmful to crop up just before the election. Had to listen to the polls!

It was a nerve-racking time for Michael. He found it nearly impossible to focus on his work or anything else. That's because he expected the police to confront him at any moment. He had no way of knowing that DD-W had decided against outing him. Michael couldn't visit Richard in the hospital or even call him on a burner phone. He felt sure that Morgan was being heavily monitored. AA called my private phone on his burner. I figured he was the unknown caller and asked, "What's up Michael?"

"I'm going out of my freaking mind, 'Rambo,' that's what!"

"Calm down, my friend. Let's talk. Get it off your chest and relax."

"Relax? How in the hell am I supposed to relax? The cops could knock on my door as we speak! What should I do?"

"Don't do anything, Michael."

"Easy for you to say!"

"Worrying won't help anything. This is the time for cooler heads to prevail." Something in the tone of my voice must have helped because Michael sighed but continued to listen. "Do you think I haven't been going crazy too?" I asked rhetorically. "I haven't had contact with anyone either, until now." Realizing that my tension had built up too, I exhaled. "I'm really glad you called. Don't forget, we're all in this together."

"Yeah, I know. I didn't mean to overlook you. What should we do?"

"Nothing, absolutely nothing. I know that's tough right now but we have no choice." Michael groaned helplessly. "Listen, I've been out of contact with you two but I'm a reporter. I still have my sources."

"What, what did you hear?"

"It's what I didn't hear. There's no word on the street about you being outed or tied to the supposed drug-deal-gone-bad involving Richard.

I don't know why but, for some reason, it seems like Darnell-Wright has decided not to sing."

Michael sounded relieved, "That's good to hear. So, we just sit?"

"Yes, sit tight and wait. Once Richard is released from the hospital, I'm sure he'll bring us up to speed."

Sure enough, a couple of days later, Richard set up a late-night meeting at our favorite rendezvous. He gingerly got out of his car, limped to the trunk and pulled out a folding chair and a big rubber donut. Richard fidgeted until the sore, healing wound was in the donut's sweet spot. Michael tried to make light of the situation, "Hemorrhoids?"

Richard grunted as he sat down, "Not funny. Now, I WILL call you a pain in the ass." We all got a good laugh.

"Want a beer?" I asked.

"Have you got anything stronger, like a slug of bourbon?"

"No, but I can go get some."

"I'm just kidding. Trust me, I'm flying high enough with these meds I'm on. Speaking of which, let's make this quick before I fall asleep. Can't wait to get back into bed – on my stomach."

I tried my best to accommodate him, "Okay, boss, the floor's all yours."

"Here's the deal. To make a long story, short, it's a good news/bad news situation."

Michael groaned, "Oh, oh."

"Here's the good news. You're in the clear, Michael. Darnell-Wright hasn't fingered you. My guess is that he still wants to take you out personally while steering clear of being held accountable for Sally."

I chirped, "That is good news."

Michael asked warily, "And the bad news?" Richard paused for a long time and struggled to find the right words. "This MUST be bad." Richard remained mute with a pained expression on his face. "C'mon man, just spit it out!"

"They're onto me." Our jaws dropped. He tried to sound casual. "I thought I dodged the bullet." We listened, confused. "Darnell-Wright must have friends on the inside because one of my own ratted me out. He didn't identify you, Michael, but he tied me to AA. They wanted to hang me out to dry for your supposed crimes. But I was able to come up with a plausible excuse. My story held up because there was no evidence to contradict my version of a drug-deal-gone-bad."

I asked, "Then what's the bad news?"

"Apparently, the prosecutor's office has had an eye on me for quite some time. They've been building up to this slowly but surely. I thought the case was closed and we were in the clear but the damn witch got suspicious and asked for ballistics. When the results showed that the slugs came from someone else's gun, they put on the full-court press."

Michael's voice wavered, "What should I do? Should I get out of town?"

"Not so fast. Relax. I didn't say I caved, did I?" Michael's eyes glimmered with fresh hope. "I didn't give you up and I'm not about to."

My reporter's instincts twitched, "What will happen to you?"

"At best, I'll lose my pension and be out of a job."

"And at worst?"

"They'll try to bring me up on charges." Our hearts sank. "Chin up, boys. They'll have a tough time making their case, especially without corroborating testimony from DD-W." He paused and smiled reassuringly, "Even if Darnell-Wright flipped, I wouldn't give you up. The cause is too great – and I believe in it wholeheartedly."

Michael offered a steely stare with his jaw set tight. "You won't have to worry about the 'King' flipping since I'll get to him first."

"No! That's the last thing we need. You've got to lay low and let this thing play out."

Michael spoke with granite resolve, "Forget it, Richard. I'm not going to even pretend to go along with you this time. It's now or never."

"Michael, no, I can't help you this time. Even if I didn't have my ass in a sling, I couldn't chance getting caught red-handed lending aid to, in their words, a criminal fugitive from the law."

"Don't need any help."

"The chances of you catching him alone are next to nothing. And they'll be armed to the teeth."

"I guess that's the chance I'll have to take. In for a penny, in for a pound."

Richard seemed to accept that the train had left the station; a freight train named AA that couldn't be stopped. In a show of support, Richard unleashed his own banality that inadvertently ignited a cliché contest. "Yeah, you've got to bet big to win big."

Michael retorted, "Go big or go home."

Richard snickered as he shot back, "You can't race a Maserati on a dirt track."

Feeling left out, I chimed in with the only thing that came to mind, "A fine cage doesn't feed the bird."

They both looked at me crosswise and snorted with glee. Seeing them doubled over and shaking uncontrollably sucked me into a three-way fit of silly chortling. When we finally came to our senses, Richard took on his serious cop glare and turned to Michael, "Don't get caught in another trap. This guy's clever as hell – and meaner than a wounded water moccasin." He paused and I could sense the gears in his head were spinning wildly. "Try to get to him before he gets to you." Michael nodded dutifully. "Catch him alone."

"I'll do my best. Hey, let's get out of here. Time's wasting."

Like a nervous father sending his son out to face down the town bully, Richard couldn't let go. "Try to get him on your turf. Or at least neutral turf." Michael nodded as he turned to jump in his car and leave. Richard kept on, "Make sure you're packing."

"Yeah, yeah, I hear you."

"I'm serious, don't get caught in a gun fight with a pea shooter."

"Okay, dad," Michael chided.

Richard looked at me with pleading eyes. "Hey, I don't own a gun and I sure as hell don't know karate." He looked desperate, almost helpless so, I turned to Michael. "Do you want me to tag along for moral support?"

Michael laughed indignantly, "Moral support I don't need." He smiled peacefully as he turned the ignition, "Just keep doing what you do best. Get the truth out there." He waved as he drove away, "Wish me luck, boys."

Richard glanced at me squeamishly, "He's going to need more than luck."

"Yeah. Right now; he needs our prayers."

As we were about to follow Michael back toward civilization, a pair of headlights came around the curve down at the end of the deserted road. A rush of high-octane adrenaline made my heart lurch. It pounded at a dizzying rate that made my head float. Richard shouted, "Kill your engine!"

I pleaded, "Who could THAT be?"

Richard tried to be optimistic but couldn't hide his anxiety. The edge in his voice betrayed his dread. "I hope it's somebody that works at the paintball park."

That hope was dashed when the beams drew closer. I offered my own wishful thinking, "Maybe some kids are coming down here to make out. Or someone's dumping their trash." Neither seemed very likely so, I looked to Richard for help. "Should we make a run for it?"

"No. If it's a cop, that would only make things worse." He tried to reassure me, "Don't worry. Just let me do the talking. I'll think of something."

Now, the car was close enough that we could hear the crunch of loose asphalt under the tires and had to shade our eyes from the blinding beams. Sweat bubbles magically appeared and beaded my forehead. I thought a blood vessel might pop when I heard a cheerful voice cry out, "Hey, I'm glad I caught you guys before you took off." It was Michael!

Richard barked, "What are you doing back here?"

"I've got an idea I want to run by you."

Richard oozed sarcasm, "Oh, you've got an idea, do you, Einstein?" Michael must have sensed Richard needed to vent so; he kept his mouth shut. "Give me a second before you share this great brainstorm with us, if you don't mind. I need to clean the crap out of my drawers."

"Sorry guys but it really is a good idea." We waited skeptically, not expecting much. "We need to strike while the iron is hot, right?" Richard and I nodded. "We want to catch him off guard, on our turf, right?" Again, we nodded. "Then, we should pick the time and place."

With fresh sarcasm, Richard challenged Michael, "Pray tell, how do you plan on delivering this invitation to 'Mr. King?'"

Michael turned to me, "That's where you come in." I stared back, baffled. "You can get the word out on the radio."

Richard huffed, "Oh, we'll just broadcast where the Avenging Angel will be over the radio? That's good – very good, genius boy!"

Michael was undeterred, "No, no – we'll say it in code so that only DD-W will understand."

This seemed to intrigue Richard who adopted a much more open tone, "Tell me more."

"We'll pick a place that only he will recognize."

"Such as?"

"Two blocks down from the first place we met. Nobody knows but him, us and three dead guys."

"Hmmmm. You know, that might just work. But why two blocks down?"

"Because there's video surveillance in the parking garage. Two blocks away there's a nice, dark alley where we can have our," he paused as if describing a forbidden pleasure, "PRIVACY," he stretched out the word. "Plus, it would be difficult for him to stage an ambush there."

I was curious, "How will we know if he's listening?"

Richard's cop-brain was way ahead of me and he answered for Michael enthusiastically. "Where else would he go? You're the only guy in town that has access to the Avenging Angel. He's trying to track down AA so, I'm betting he's a regular listener."

A puzzled look crimped Michael's face. "He knows who I am. Can't he find me at work or where I live?"

"Of course, but he doesn't want any connection to you or Sally. He wants to get a line on your whereabouts as the Avenging Angel and catch you in the act. If he can take you out as AA, that is, if you're killed in action so to speak, the press would treat it as karma. They'd have a field day reporting how a ruthless vigilante got his just deserts. By the time they've identified AA as Michael Wyatt, motive would already have been established by the media in the court of public opinion. No one would ever know your death was actually the result of a personal vendetta that could be traced back to Darnell-Wright."

I added, "Makes sense, Richard. But what if you're wrong. What if DD-W doesn't show?

Michael answered, "If not, what have we lost? I'll know if he was listening if he shows up."

Richard zinged us with one more string of clichés before we all left. "One shot, a shot in the dark, maybe our last shot is better than no shot at all."

Chapter 16:

Having a workable plan buoyed Michael's spirits but, by the next evening after a painfully slow day at work, he had second thoughts. The gravity of the situation weighed heavily on his heart and soul. Michael realized the odds were not in his favor. There was a good chance that he might forfeit his life in this last-ditch effort to seek justice for Sally. Although he tried to block it out, he couldn't help but think, *is it worth it? Sally's gone for all intents and purposes.* His conflicted brain bellowed, *NO! Her spirit is still alive and well, in God's care. Is it worth it? Hell YES!*

He knew he had to visit Sally, perhaps for the last time. It was much more than setting up his perfect alibi by climbing out the window and stealing down the side of the building. His bond to Sally was as strong as ever. It didn't matter that she couldn't speak to him. He had to talk to her. Michael desperately needed to share his feelings. He wanted to call upon God in prayer on her behalf in her presence.

He had planned things just right to allow time before heading off to his rendezvous with destiny. The nurse on duty had just left from her last round until midnight. He held Sally's hand that was still limp but encouragingly warm. Michael gazed at Sally's face. To him, it was still a thing of beauty even though she had grown pale and gaunt due to months of inactivity. Michael didn't dwell on the wear and tear their ordeal with Darnell-Wright and his evil friends had inflicted upon her. He thought, *thank you, Almighty God, for this beautiful creation.*

Still clasping her hand, Michael knelt beside her bed and prayed. "Dear Lord, Heavenly Father, how many times have I lifted my petitions before you on Sally's behalf? My old, sinful self would have me believe that you're not listening. But thank you, Lord, that I have not given into doubt because I have your sure word of promise in the Bible. Thank you for blessing me with patience. I know that you've heard me and will fulfill your good and gracious will in your perfect time."

He bowed his head even lower, "Yet, here I am again, Lord. I come before you pleading for healing and comfort and restoration, knowing full well that all things are possible with you. While you walked the earth, you demonstrated your miraculous healing power over and over again. Lord, you even raised people from the dead. Thus, I place my faith and trust in you; faith and trust fortified in the resurrection of our Lord and Savior, Jesus Christ."

Michael drew his hand and Sally's closer, over his heart. "My desire is to be reunited with my precious wife in the fullness of life. Please guide, bless and protect her physicians and nurses that they might effectually administer your care. Moreover, please reach out and touch Sally with your caring, loving and all-powerful, healing and creative hand. Please bless our marriage that we might continue to grow in our love toward one another and our Lord and Savior, Jesus Christ."

He brought his other hand in and clasped Sally's hand between his two. "Although this is my fondest desire, still I pray in this as in all things that thy will be done, for you always know what is best for us. Our trust is in you alone, Lord. For we know that you are working all things together for good to them that love you; to them who are the called according to your purpose. Whether in this life or the next, I know that I will see Sally again, full of vigor and vitality and new life in mind, body and spirit."

Michael reverently leaned forward to surround Sally's hand with his hands and forehead. "Dear Lord, I am a sinful human being. The very best works I have to offer are horribly tainted with sin. Thus, I pray, please sanctify me to know and do thy will as I embark on a dangerous mission. Help me to seek justice rather than vengeance. Protect me from Satan and his minions. Please watch over me and send your holy angels to watch over me. Most importantly, please guide me down the path of righteousness and help me to follow Christ's example. In Jesus precious name I pray, amen."

Michael heaved a peaceful sigh of relief as he gently replaced Sally's hand over her other one. Filled with the confidence that can only come through faith and trust in the Lord, he stretched his arms, legs and back as if preparing for an athletic competition. After opening the window and dropping the rope down the dark corner of the building, he pivoted back to kiss Sally one last time. Turning to leave, he halted abruptly to offer one last prayer. "Lord, although I'm willing to lay it down, I pray that you will preserve my life. However, if I die, please continue to watch over Sally."

When Michael opened his eyes, he saw something that astonished him. For only a split second, if that, it appeared that Sally's eyelids had fluttered. Could it be? Had her eyeballs twitched back and forth wildly at the prospect of his death? He stared at her intently, looking for any sign of recognition. Alas, there was nothing but the gentle, almost imperceptible heaving of her chest as air passed in and out of her lungs.

Michael convinced himself he'd been seeing things, wishful thinking. Still, it left him with a creeping doubt; the last thing he needed at a time like this.

I had followed Michael's instructions to a T. Not only did I mention on my show the specific clues that would lead Darnell-Wright to the exact location but cautioned him emphatically to come alone. None of us believed he'd follow those instructions so, Michael arrived plenty early and positioned himself where he could scope out the entrance before entering the alleyway. As anticipated, the "King" brought two of his loyal subjects along. They slipped into an alley on the other side of the street. Apparently, the plan was for them to wait and follow AA in after he'd confronted DD-W, supposedly one-on-one.

Michael foiled their nefarious plan by following the two gangbangers into the other alley. He got the drop on them before they could even pull out their guns. With vicious but quiet efficiency, he dispatched both of them into la-la land with a flurry of kicks and punches that overwhelmed the two thugs. Having evened the odds, he drew his gun and slipped into the opposing alleyway. His first words rang with lethal practicality, "Give me your gun."

Darnell-Wright obliged without a hint of worry. Michael felt delicious satisfaction as he tried to wipe the smirk off DD-W's face, "By the way, 'King,'" he spat derisively, "I've already taken care of your backups. It's just you and me."

Oddly, this didn't seem to bother the grinning thug in the least. "You're a pretty good chess player, Mr. AA," he waved his hand theatrically toward the entrance to the alley, "But I'd say this is checkmate." The wily hoodlum had outflanked Michael by anticipating that he'd somehow ferret out the first two backups and neutralize them. He'd assigned two other goons to arrive even earlier and wait in the wings until AA actually entered the alley. DD-W ordered, "Take those guns away from him."

Michael knew his goose was cooked. He said a silent prayer while trying to maintain a calm exterior, *God, I'm in trouble. I need your help. Please make your strength perfect in my weakness.* He tried to engage his hated nemesis to buy time and, hopefully, get him to let his guard down. "Too bad. I was hoping for a little friendly competition, mano-a-mano." DD-W laughed casually with the ease of a man in total control. "But hey, congratulations, you outfoxed me. You won fair and square."

The jovial thug mocked Michael, "Thank you, man. I'm glad to see you're taking it so well."

Michael appealed, "Now that we're such good friends, can you do me one small favor?"

He seemed to enjoy the repartee as he played along, "Sure AA, just name it, bruh."

Michael feigned sadness, regret and fear, "Can you make it quick?"

Darnell-Wright flashed a wicked grin as he massaged his chin, "I'm sorry man. Anything but that. Cigarette, a cold beer, one last taco – but not that. No can do." He dropped the façade and turned back into the cold, ruthless killer that had attacked Sally so viciously. "Naw, you got some payback coming before we finna shoot yo sorry ass."

Michael egged him on since his only chance was to get physical before guns entered into the equation. Now assertive, he threw down, "You want to talk about payback? My wife is still in the hospital, wasting away like a damn vegetable, thanks to you!"

"Yeah, let's talk about payback. Yo white ass gonna get what's coming to you for 'Beast,' 'Onion' and 'Lil C.'" He glared at Michael with sinister, soulless eyes; the eyes of a sadist; the eyes of a demon. "Just remember this, Mr. Angel. After yo dead, I'm gone fix that little wife of yours. Pick up where I left off. Only, this time, I'll finish the job."

Michael lowered his chin while shooting imaginary daggers from his eyes, "Bring it on, punk."

"Hold 'em," he ordered as he advanced slowly, dukes up. This was just what Michael wanted. The goons on either side of him stuck their guns into their waistbands and seized him roughly and firmly by his arms. Michael offered minimal resistance as he braced for the onslaught. DD-W stopped abruptly, pointed to the thug on Michael's left and snapped, "Check his pockets." They found what the "King" wanted; a Duracell AA battery affixed with little paper wings. "Gimme that." He grinned before grimacing threateningly, "Yo gone eat this, AA."

Michael took it like a human punching bag as DD-W attempted to slowly take him apart. First, a couple of stiff jabs split his lip. Then a solid punch to the gut doubled Michael over. Next, the thug gleefully delivered an arcing roundhouse that exploded across the side of Michael's face. With blood streaming from his nose, lips and ear,

Michael slumped as if the last blow had turned out the lights. That wasn't enough to satisfy DD-W's devilish bloodlust. "Hold him up. Ain't through by a longshot!"

This was the moment of truth; do or die. One of the thugs grabbed Michael by the hair to set his head upright while the other heaved to stand him up straight. Using that momentum, Michael sprang to life, threw his head back violently and tucked his knees tightly into his chest. In a scene that could have made Jackie Chan proud, Michael turned a complete back flip that left him directly behind the two goons. He placed the palms of his hands on the outsides of their heads and, as if doing chest flies in the gym, slammed their noggins together with enough force to crack open a couple of coconuts.

Totally disoriented, they couldn't react. Michael locked his fingers behind the head of the bigger of the two and pulled down hard as he simultaneously thrust his knee up into the man's jaw. Then, with an acrobatic move like something out of the WWE, Michael thrust his hips skyward and locked his thighs around the skull of the other hoodlum. Twisting violently, he generated incredible centrifugal force. With the aid of gravity, his lower extremities returned to earth in a horrific crash landing with the unfortunate goon's crown taking the brunt of the damage.

While Michael dispatched the two enforcers, Darnell-Wright quickly seized the opportunity to make a play for one of the discarded handguns. Just as he gripped the lethal weapon, Michael reacted like an Olympic gymnast with a perfect kip-up to regain his footing. DD-W whirled, gun in hand, to find his mark. Michael Wyatt didn't have time to see his life flash before his eyes. He wasn't quite close enough to strike a blow to disarm his bloodthirsty antagonist.

It was as if God slowed down time or perhaps an unseen guardian angel offered an assist. Somehow, Michael was so locked in that he recognized the muzzle flash a nano-second before the loud report. While this occurred, the Avenging Angel bent backwards outrageously, limbo-style, like a scene from the *Matrix*. The round came so close to his supine chest that he could feel the heat against his skin. As it zipped past, within an inch of his head, the bullet buzzed like a bumble bee from hell.

Before the "King" could fire again, Michael performed another maneuver that seemed almost humanly impossible. Momentarily suspended in air, parallel to the ground, he whipped his right leg upward from his left as if he were a soccer player executing a perfect bicycle kick. His foot slapped against DD-W's hand, kicking the gun straight up into the air. As if the stunned thug wasn't astonished enough, Michael landed crab-style on his feet and hands. Immediately, he straightened up into a standing position, thrust his hand skyward and snagged the gun before it could hit the ground.

Still reeling from the incredible turn of events that put him at AA's mercy, DD-W stretched out his hands and pleaded, "Don't shoot! Please!"

Michael glared with deadly intent, offering no mercy to the suddenly contrite criminal. "Spare you so you can finish off my wife?"

"I'm sorry! I'm sorry for everything!" He actually cried. "I can change! I really can," he pleaded.

There wasn't a hint of mercy in Michael's steely reply, "And the Academy Award goes to."

"I'm serious, man!"

"Of course, you are, *Ebeneezer*. Now, do you want me to buy that big Christmas turkey for *Tiny Tim*?"

Darcy Darnell-Wright was reduced to blubbering. He became so sloppy that a snot bubble popped out of his left nostril. "I will make it up to you! Somehow, I will!"

This sent Michael over the edge. Seething rage gripped him as if he were demon-possessed. "You'll make it up to me? You'll make it up to me?" his voice thundered. "Are you going to raise your three buddies from the grave before or after you miraculously heal my wife?" His voice trembled with hatred as he roared one last command, "Down on your knees!"

Now, genuinely fearing for his life, Darnell-Wright said nothing as he knelt on the hard pavement. Michael stepped closer and took aim at the quivering thug's forehead from point-blank range. DD-W stuttered pitifully, "Don't shoot."

"This is my contribution to the betterment of mankind; worthless piece of."

"Stop!" bellowed a voice behind Michael.

Michael stepped back, out of range of DD-W's armlength, while keeping his Glock trained on the thug's head. He had recognized the voice but turned his head just enough to verify Richard's presence. "Don't interfere."

Morgan tried to reason with his friend but he was talking to a brick wall. "You've never murdered anyone. It's always been in defense of yourself or someone else."

"Don't waste your breath."

"Do you want to become a murderer?"

"This sorry excuse for a human being, this animal, has threatened to kill Sally – to finish the job as he put it. So no, I don't consider it murder to defend Sally's life."

"Michael, it would never stand up in court. You don't have to murder him to protect Sally."

"I'm not willing to take that chance." He focused even more intently on DD-W while moving in closer for the kill.

Sensing he wouldn't listen, I jumped in, "Michael, don't do it. You're not a murderer!"

"Call it what you want. You say murder, I say justice. Justice for Sally!"

"Michael, please listen. Sally doesn't want this kind of justice."

This caused him to pause momentarily. But then his anger rose, "Oh, she doesn't, does she?"

He must have contemplated her lying helpless in her bed, dead to the world for all intents and purposes. "Are you clairvoyant, 'Rambo?'" he spat mockingly.

Richard hit him with this stunner, "No, Michael, she told us."

Michael didn't take his eyes off Darnell-Wright for a second as he scolded us, "That's really low. You're so concerned about this piece of human excrement that you'd lie about Sally to save his miserable life? Despicable!"

Richard tried to explain, "It's not a lie. We just came from the med center. She regained consciousness."

I confirmed it, "It's true. It was like a miracle." For the first time, there was a hint of humanity in Michael's eyes. "We would never lie to you about something like this." I added this detail for authenticity, "By the way, we took care of that rope for you before anyone discovered it."

Michael stepped back far enough to where he could keep one eye on DD-W while simultaneously inspecting us. "She talked to you?"

"Yes," I declared.

"Okay, what did she say?"

Richard spoke, "We told her about our plan. She said she knew you were risking your life to seek justice for her."

Michael muttered under his breath, "So, she did hear me!"

Richard continued, "She became very distraught and said she just wanted you back. Sally said she didn't care about justice. She just wanted you back."

Michael spoke in a softer tone, "Thank you! Thank you for this incredible, miraculous news. And thank you, Lord! Thank you for hearing my prayers!"

Richard coaxed him, "Okay, Michael, give me the gun. Let's go see Sally."

Michael grimaced like a man truly torn, "Yes, let's go see Sally but, first, I've got to deal with this devil."

I tried to derail what remained a deadly freight train, "Sally doesn't want that! She just wants you." He seemed unaffected by my plea. "Sally has forgiven Darnell-Wright!"

"Well, she's a better person than me." He paused to reflect as a wicked grin emerged. "I'll forgive him too – just before I blow him away." I folded my hands in prayer and looked at Michael with desperate, pleading eyes. "I'm sorry but I can't take any more chances with Sally's life. I've got to eliminate the threat."

Richard made a last-ditch effort, "Sally asked us to deliver a message to you, 'Don't let hate conquer love.'"

Michael paused, totally conflicted now. I added, "She quoted Ephesians 4:32, 'And be ye kind one to another, tenderhearted, forgiving one another, even as God for Christ's sake hath forgiven you.' Michael, do it for Christ's sake."

This must have hit home. I imagined that Michael pictured Jesus Christ suffering on the Cross of Calvary to pay the infinite, ultimate price for all our sins. He lowered the gun and exhaled, "What was I thinking? Please forgive me, Lord."

The Spirit moved us all, that is, except for Satan's spawn, Darcy Darnell-Wright. While Michael's attention was diverted, he reached down under his pant leg where a .22 was strapped just above his ankle. Michael was helpless, paying no attention to his nemesis. However,

Richard's cop-mind was fully engaged despite sharing our joy. DD-W was so quick at raising the gun and firing that Richard's only option was to reflexively throw his body in front of Michael.

The shot was deafening as it echoed off the high brick walls in the narrow alleyway. In the noise and confusion, Michael remained hopelessly defenseless as a second shot rang out.

Epilogue:

Just before the Christmas break, I devoted the entire two-hour broadcast to a commemoration of AA's life and legacy. After recounting the saga, I was able to summarize with a few life lessons that were made clearer through 20/20, or should I say 2020 hindsight. "Good morning listeners! We have a special treat for you today. We're going to devote the entire show to that one anonymous guy who stood up for us all during one of the worst years in our nation's history. Yes, we salute the one, the only, drum roll please, Avenging Angel. May he rest in peace.

"Thank God that 2020 is almost over. But will 2021 be any different? I thought so on election night until the vote counting stopped in key battleground states just when it appeared that President Trump's re-election was certain. Even the mobs thought it was curtains for Biden when they prematurely started burning and looting. I remember saying on air that we could have used another Avenging Angel when the riots broke out."

I laughed out loud while recalling the utter insanity of it all. "Excuse me for busting up but I couldn't help thinking about the Democrat mantra during the 2020 campaign. Remember how they bombarded the President with questions about the peaceful transition of power? Talk about the pot calling the kettle black! They'd been resisting the results of the 2016 election for four years! When late-night shenanigans threw the 2020 election results into total confusion, they claimed victory while demanding that the President's campaign concede. Someone forgot to send the memo to the goon squads though. They rioted as if they'd been overcome by the President's red wave.

"I really got a kick out of the warnings just before election day. Remember how quite a few stores in a number of our large cities boarded up the windows with plywood in anticipation of more rioting and looting? The Demon-Rats claimed they were bracing for Trump's sore losers. Funny how many of the store owners were spray painting 'We Support BLM' on the plywood. Yeah right! All of us Trump supporters would have been appeased by that. Gimme a break!

"Biden's sore losers rioted all right but thankfully it petered out quickly when the vote counting recommenced. Magically, hundreds of thousands of ballots materialized out of thin air. Never mind that some batches contained ballots cast 100% for Joe Biden, a statistical impossibility. Many were marked only for Biden with no other down-ballot offices or election measures marked beyond president. They didn't bother or have the time to vote for the House and Senate candidates? It didn't matter that postmarks were changed and outer envelopes bearing fake signatures or no signatures at all were discarded. What looked like a Trump landslide somehow became a Biden victory. Or at least that's what the media declared.

"Yeah, since when did the media get to certify the results of our elections? It must have been the same time that someone decided that state officials and judges got to change voting laws rather than state legislatures. Forget the Constitution, they said. There was just one problem. Did they really think Donald Trump would back down from a fight? He resisted every call for a so-called unity concession. He exercised every legal right under the Constitution to contest the rigged election.

"The media went berserk, including all the libs and RINO cowards at Fox News. The Dems resorted to win-at-all-cost coercion. They had no choice given the alternative of stiff jail time for voter fraud on top of all their other criminal conspiracies. First, they tried blatant cover-ups by barring Republicans from observing counts and recounts. Then they attacked whistleblowers even threatening them and their families with violence or death. The swampy Post Office was complicit too. They went so far as to punish postal workers who refused to recant their eyewitness testimony of systematic voter fraud.

"The media gathered themselves in time to endlessly repeat the narrative that there was NO EVIDENCE of voter fraud. As tons of evidence surfaced, they changed their mantra to NOT ENOUGH EVIDENCE to affect the outcome of the election. The calls for unity became frantic. They claimed that the President's refusal to concede was unprecedented. Somehow, they forgot how their guy, Al Gore, had contested the outcome of the 2000 election for well over a month all the way up to the Supreme Court.

"When all else failed, they unleashed their Antifa and BLM storm troopers again. It came to a head when President Trump's supporters staged a million-person march in Washington, D. C. in mid-November. It truly was a peaceful protest but that didn't matter. Of course, the cowardly anarchists didn't dare confront the throngs of citizens exercising their First Amendment rights in broad daylight. They waited until darkness fell to attack innocent stragglers once the thugs had the advantage in numbers. Do you remember me invoking the good old days when we could count on AA to stand up for the rest of us?

"As we sit here, there's plenty of credible evidence that the software behind Dominion voting machines was manipulated to automatically switch votes from Trump to Biden. And this was programmed in BEFORE the election even took place! Hello Venezuela! The plan was messed up by the unanticipated size of Trump's red wave. That's why the counting was stopped; so that they could reprogram the software to come up with more votes for Biden. I know it sounds crazy but that's what is bubbling up to probably the Supreme Court right now.

"Yes, everything is still up in the air including the so-called deadly pandemic. Will we ever get back to normal? Can we get back to not only working hard but playing hard? When can we have schools opened and Little League parks and professional stadiums filled? In 2021 will we be able to celebrate Mardi Gras, St. Patrick's Day, Easter and the Fourth of July? And without those dreadful masks? Most importantly, will we be able to shout hallelujah and open our churches for worship without freaking social distancing?

"Thankfully, even in the midst of the election chaos, we've seen a few signs of sanity returning.

Remember when the crazies on the Minneapolis City Council voted to defund the police? As any sane person could have predicted, crime went through the roof. Last month, a few semi-lucid members of the Council voted to spend $500,000 to hire some rent-a-cops to try to stop the bleeding. Still, the madness persists in places like Portland and all the other sanctuary cities. Would anything help cesspools like San Francisco? That's where we need someone like AA the most.

"I doubt that even he could help today. We've become a nation of idiots! Tell the truth, people. Did you cancel Thanksgiving due to the likes of 'Witchy' Witmer, 'Coo-Coo' Cuomo and 'Heinrich Himmler' Newsom? Really, you listened to Gadabout Gavin who feasted lavishly at an indoor, fine-dining establishment without a mask with some corrupt lobbyists while he ordered you to eat outside while wearing a mask? Really? C'mon, people! Now, they want you to wear a mask inside your own house! MASKS DON'T WORK, you morons!

"Sorry for losing my cool but the insanity has reached a new level that I thought was impossible. Remember when I predicted that the pandemic fearmongering would end on election day? I was dead wrong because I couldn't foresee the depth of the voter fraud that the Dems would brazenly deploy. So, we're still stuck with the COVID crisis. In fact, in places like right here in St. Louis, we're back in lockdown mode. Some people never learn. Yet, somehow, President Trump's V-shaped economic recovery is still running full-speed ahead. Thankfully, just as he promised, his project Warp Speed produced multiple vaccines just in time. Once again, he delivered even more than he promised with Pfizer and Moderna offering vaccines with effectivity rates above 90% even though fraudulent-Fauci said we should only expect 50% at best.

"What a shot in the arm for the economy and the stock market!" I couldn't contain some laughter. "See what I did folks? Vaccine? Shot in the arm?" I chuckled some more. "Of course, some of the loons still resisted. Governor Cuomo in New York vowed not to allow the Trump vaccine into his state. That is, until the President went on air to lament that New Yorkers wouldn't be able to get the vaccine. Then the Governor howled that President Trump was withholding the vaccine. You can't make this stuff up, folks! All I can say is, too bad that Pfizer and Moderna conveniently waited until AFTER the election to break this great news. I guess the President was right again when he said Big Pharma hated him for making them lower their exorbitant drug prices to all Americans. But I digress.

"Let me get back to the matter at hand, dear listeners. At this point in the story, you must be convinced that AA died at the hands of Darcy Darnell-Wright. I'm sorry if I misled you when I said may he rest in peace. However, I have good news for you. I was referring to the persona of the Avenging Angel and not the man behind it. He's alive and well but has retired from the crusading crimefighter business. For obvious reasons, I can't reveal his identity. But I can tell you that he survived and moved on.

"How did he survive that stare-down with an armed, vicious killer at point blank range? Unfortunately, I can't share any details that might compromise AA's privacy. However, I can tell you this much. AA owes his life to a hero of another sort, a hero in blue who, by chance, happened onto the scene by, I suppose, the providence of God. His name is Officer Richard Morgan."

I went on to provide my radio audience with a synopsis of the events in that dark alley that led to the death of Darcy Darnell-Wright. As background, I provided the truth about AA's true character, that he suffered personal tragedies at the hands of riotous criminals and followed altruistic motives in trying to protect others in harm's way. However, I couldn't tell them everything, including specific details, without jeopardizing Richard's or Michael and Sally's futures. So, I only shared the bare-boned truth that DD-W was killed in self-defense during a shootout with a courageous cop; a cop who only knew the Avenging Angel by reputation and not his true identity.

Here are the details that were only known by me, Michael Wyatt and Richard Morgan. As stated previously, it was true that AA spared DD-W's life after hearing of Sally's plea. Yes, he almost forfeited his own life by showing mercy to DD-W. But Richard Morgan did, in fact, take a bullet for Michael Wyatt. How did they both survive? Let's go back to that fateful night for the full story.

When Officer Richard Morgan dove in front of the bullet headed for Michael, it struck him center-mass where he was protected by his Kevlar vest. It saved his life but the force of the bullet put Richard momentarily out of commission at that crucial moment. When I asked him later what if felt like he replied, "Words can't describe it. If you really want to know, let me take a swing at your chest with a sledge-hammer." In any case,

Richard was in no position to stop Darnell-Wright from firing another round at Michael who stood defenseless as the cop writhed on the ground.

That's where I came in. Although I'd never owned or fired a gun in my life before I met him, Richard had prodded me into borrowing one of his back-up service revolvers. Then he personally trained me on how to use the thing at a local shooting range. At Richard's insistence, I brought it along that night as we broke our vow to Michael to not interfere. It wasn't so much that we doubted Michael's skill and resolve but we knew how evil and dangerous DD-W could be. We hung back watching through a window above street-level but scrambled to serve as his reinforcements as soon as we spied the second set of goons heading toward the alley.

Never in my life would I have guessed I could wield a deadly weapon, much less fire a gun at another human being. But when DD-W shot Richard, some deep-down survival instinct kicked in. I pointed and fired at Darnell-Wright before he could blast hot lead into Michael's forehead. It was ironic that the Avenging Angel was moved by the Savior's word from Scripture to forgive Darcy Darnell-Wright, as he'd been forgiven by the Lord, only to have me, someone who'd just pleaded for him to show mercy, serve up justice in such a violent way.

The others were only unconscious – the two in the other alley were either still out cold or had slunk away to lick their wounds – but DD-W was dead so, we decided to call the police and turn ourselves in. However, Michael argued that there was no need for all three of us to take the fall since the two thugs laying on the ground had been knocked cold before Richard and I arrived on the scene. He surmised, "This is still on me. I'm the Avenging Angel. I'll take the rap." We tried to object but he was adamant. "This whole thing, my crusade against crime, was my baby from start to finish. It's time for me to come clean and face the consequences."

Richard objected, "All for one and one for all. We knew what we were getting into when we threw in with you."

"There's no reason for you guys to stick around. None of these guys can place you at the scene, if you hurry before they wake up." We still shook our heads. "Bucco, Richard, this is something I've got to do. It's the only way for me to clear my name and get on with life. Besides, I need someone to look after Sally until this is over."

His last statement swayed me but there was a big hurdle standing in the way. "But Michael, they're already onto Richard. His goose is cooked either way."

Richard stopped me, "Wait, there's something I haven't shared with you yet. It just broke today. By some miracle, I'm free and clear."

I couldn't believe my ears, "What are you talking about? You said they had you dead to rights; that, best case, you'd lose your badge and pension."

"That's right but I don't know how to explain it other than God must have intervened." We stared blankly with our mouths agape. "Apparently, the Governor's office initiated an investigation into the City Prosecutor's office months ago. This afternoon, they lowered the boom. It appears the Prosecutor and key members of her staff were up to their ears in corruption including bribes, malfeasance and even extortion. She and her whole crooked crew are gone. They won't be bothering me or any other cop on the force anymore."

I was too astonished to speak but Michael seized the opportunity immediately. "There, don't you see? It's God's will! And if He was there for you, He will be there for me too." He motioned us away. "Now, get out of here before any of these guys come to."

Richard countered, "Hold on man. Even though it was self-defense, you'd have a tough time in court. I'd have a much stronger case."

I couldn't contain myself, "But I'm the one who shot him!"

"True, but when they run the ballistics, they'll see that the bullet came from my gun." I frowned but Richard wouldn't be deterred. "Look at how the evidence stacks up. He shot me and I shot him. It's an open and shut case."

Michael offered a challenge, "But what about those guys and the other two across the street?"

Richard reasoned, "So what? They will report that they got their butts kicked by the Avenging Angel. Still, they won't be able to identify you. It all comes down to me taking a bullet for you and then killing Darnell-Wright." He paused and added, "I came upon the scene by chance, saved your butt and then you took off before I could apprehend and identify you."

Michael still objected, "But that's not true."

Richard grinned mischievously, "Maybe I'm stretching the truth a bit but it's essentially what happened with a few slight modifications necessary to protect you guys." Michael and I started to protest further but Richard stopped us in our tracks. "Look guys, this wouldn't be possible if it weren't for the Governor stepping in to get rid of that corrupt prosecutor and her slimy crew. That's God's hand at work. He's made a way of escape for all of us."

Maybe it didn't show a lot of valor on our part to leave Richard holding the bag but we weren't about to chance being on the wrong side of God. After all, we couldn't think of any other explanation for the incredible, miraculous circumstances that had occurred in the nick of time. So, we put our trust in God that He would see Richard through any investigation into the killing of DD-W.

As it turned out, providence WAS on our side. Richard was cleared of any wrongdoing and DD-W's death was ruled to be due to the justifiable use of deadly force. Michael Wyatt's identity remained anonymous and he was free to aid Sally in her recovery. I was not only spared from any consequences for my involvement but my fortunes were greatly enhanced in the process. My exclusive coverage of AA's saga garnered me national syndication.

The two-hour commemoration was a great show that set new records for ratings. By chance, there were five minutes remaining when I wrapped up my final chronicle of the amazing saga of the Avenging Angel. So, I said, "With the few minutes we have left, let's go to the phones."

As luck, or maybe misfortune, would have it, the first caller ambushed me as only he could, in his unique, staccato style. "Hey Mr. 'Rambo,' yeah, um, hey. Dis is, uh, caller Kevin. Um, remember me? I, uh, I, uh, got a question. I, uh, got a question for you, Mr. 'Rambo' there."

Somehow, I squeezed in a short reply. "How could I forget you, Kevin? Make it quick. We're almost out of time."

"Um, okay there, Mr. 'Rambo.' What, I mean, whatever, you know, whatever happened to that Avenging Angel guy. Do you? Waddaya think? I mean, do you think we'll ever see him? See him again? Huh Mr. 'Rambo?'"

I heard my producer's voice through my headphones, "Hey, he's on the phone. Says he's the Avenging Angel." I thanked Kevin for his question and asked him to listen for the answer as I cut him off.

"Oh boy, here we go. What the hell. Put him through."

To my delight, I knew it wasn't a crank call as soon as I heard Michael's voice. "Good morning, Bucco, I mean, 'Rambo!'"

"Folks, this is no joke. We have the one and only Avenging Angel on the air with us. AA, how the hell are you? Where the hell are you?"

"We're listening to your show from deep down in the heart of Texas. My lovely bride and I are doing fine. We love it down here. Of course, we miss you all back in St. Louis but, thankfully, we can livestream your program down here."

"Well, that's good to hear. Did you catch today's show?"

"The whole thing. It was great. You brought back some fantastic and a few painful memories. But all-in-all, you brought big smiles to our faces."

"It all turned out well in the end, didn't it, big boy?"

"All things work together for good to them that love God, to them who are the called according to His purpose."

"Amen, brother!"

"As for me and the wife, we're in tall cotton down here. Tucked away in the middle of nowhere with nothing but cactus and scrub as far as the eye can see. Nope, couldn't be better. But, anyway, I just wanted to say hello and thanks to all your listeners. Plus, I've got some news for you. We just welcomed a little baby girl into the world. She's as cute as a bug in a rug."

"I bet she is."

"One more thing. We have a visitor staying with us for a few days who wants to say hello."

"Who's that?"

"Let's just say he's an old pal of yours."

"Put him on."

"Hello, Bucco. How are things back in the Lou?" I recognized Richard's voice but didn't reveal his identity. "Are you keeping the streets safe up there now that AA's gone?"

"You know it, brother! Tell the truth. How are things down on AA's ranch?"

"Well, it's more of a ranch house than a ranch, but it's all good. You'd never find the place without a map and a good bloodhound. Anyway, they're treating me like a king. Mrs. AA is as beautiful as ever. I still can't believe the Angel hooked her." He sounded totally relaxed as he laughed at himself. "And this baby girl; she's an angel from heaven."

"That's awesome! Hey, we're just about out of time. Let's get together for a drink when you get back. Let me talk to AA once more."

"Will do, Bucco. Here he is."

"Hey Tex, God's blessings to you all. Real quick, please tell our listeners what you named your little girl."

Michael deadpanned, "Angel, what else?"

"No way!"

"Just kidding. But it's close. Angela."

I chortled, "Hope she follows in daddy's footsteps." My pace picked up as the last few seconds ticked away. "Before we leave, what about Kevin's question. Will we ever see the Avenging Angel again?"

Michael snickered, "I'll let you know after the election is settled and, hopefully, the craziness ends. This thing stinks to high heaven with

Benedict Barr admitting that he's been covering up the Hunter Biden bombshell since 2018. I'm guessing that, with their sham victory supposedly in hand, they'll want to impeach Biden pronto or boot him out under the 25th Amendment to make way for 'President' Harris. If the Supreme Court has been sucked into the Deep State Swamp too, I think the backlash will be much bigger than anything I could muster. I guess we'll see very soon. In the meantime, watch out for those copycats. I hear they're everywhere."

A FINAL NOTE FROM RAMBO:

Just between friends, I've got to come clean. The phone call from AA ending the show was contrived. I wasn't caught off guard, other than by caller Kevin, and it didn't come from the Lone Star State. Richard and AA were in St. Louis using an untraceable, disposable phone. The Texas ruse worked. Authorities went on a wild goose chase through the thickets, cactus and rattlers around Cotulla, Texas before giving up the hunt. Birth records didn't yield any leads either since, as you know, Michael and Sally were unable to have children. However, they did tell me they planned to adopt a little boy when the time was right. I'm not sure if they were joking when they said they planned on naming him C. B. Wyatt for Charles Bronson.

<u>Other Books by Steve Stranghoener:</u>

No Name Returns: Seven Days that Changed the World

The Seven Deadliest Lies

Uncle Sam's White Hat (No Name's 1st visit)

Faith Food: A Spiritual Smorgasbord of Daily Devotions

A Deplorable 2018 Election Guide

Deadly Preference

530 Reasons Why Deplorables Won

Veeper

Ferguson Miracle

God-Whacked!

Cha-Cha Chandler: Teen Demonologist

Straight Talk about Christian Misconceptions

The Last Prophet: Doomsday Diary

The Last Prophet: Imminent End

Murder by Chance: Blood Moon Lunacy of Lew Carew

Asunder: The Tale of the Renaissance Killer

Tracts in Time

Curious Cousins Club (Juvenile Mystery Series):

The Haunted Farmhouse

The Phantom of Pier Park

The Curious Case of the Demented Clowns

The Creature from Clingman's Dome

The Legend of the Lost Lagoon

All of these titles are available under Books/Steve Stranghoener at www.amazon.com.

Made in the USA
Monee, IL
20 February 2021